GLIMMER TRAIN
STORIES

EDITORS
Susan Burmeister-Brown
Linda Davies

CONSULTING EDITORS
Scott Allie, Annie Callan, Dave Chipps

COPY EDITOR
Mark Morris

TYPESETTING & LAYOUT
Florence McMullen

COVER ILLUSTRATOR
Jane Zwinger

STORY ILLUSTRATOR
Jon Leon

FINAL-PAGE ILLUSTRATOR
Bernard Mulligan, Republic of Ireland

PUBLISHED QUARTERLY
in February, May, August, and November by
Glimmer Train Press, Inc.
812 SW Washington Street, Suite 1205
Portland, Oregon 97205-3216 U.S.A.
Telephone: 503/221-0836
Facsimile: 503/221-0837

Glimmer Train (ISSN # 1055-7520), registered in U.S. Patent and Trademark Office, is published quarterly, $29 per year in the U.S., by Glimmer Train Press, Inc., Suite 1205, 812 SW Washington, Portland, OR 97205. Second-class postage paid at Portland, OR, and additional mailing offices. POSTMASTER: Send address changes to Glimmer Train Press, Inc., Suite 1205, 812 SW Washington, Portland, OR 97205.

ISSN # 1055-7520, ISBN # 1-880966-11-5, CPDA BIPAD # 79021

DISTRIBUTION: Bookstores can purchase *Glimmer Train Stories* through these distributors:
Anderson News Company, 9632 Hwy. 20W, Madison, AL 35728
Bernhard DeBoer, Inc., 113 E. Centre St., Nutley, NJ 07110
Bookpeople, 7900 Edgewater Dr., Oakland, CA 94621
Ingram Periodicals, 1226 Heil Quaker Blvd., LaVergne, TN 37086
IPD, 674 Via de la Valle, #204, Solana Beach, CA 92075
Pacific Pipeline, 8030 S. 228th St., Kent, WA 98032
Ubiquity, 607 Degraw St., Brooklyn, NY 11217

SUBSCRIPTION SVCS: EBSCO, Faxon, READMORE

PRINTED IN U.S.A. ON RECYCLED, ACID-FREE PAPER. ✪

Subscription rates: One year, $29 within the U.S. (Visa/MC/check). Airmail to Canada, $39; outside North America, $49. Payable by Visa/MC or check for U.S. dollars drawn on a U.S. bank.

*Attention short-story writers: We pay $500 for first publication and one-time anthology rights. Please include a self-addressed, sufficiently stamped envelope with your submission. **Manuscripts accepted in January, April, July, and October.** Send a SASE for guidelines, which will include information on our Short-Story Award for New Writers.*

*D*edication

J. LEON 94—

"Did you ever see 'Sunday in the Park with George'?
There's a marvelous song, 'A hat, a hat,
I made a hat, where there never was a hat.'
That's what art is.
You make a hat where there never was a hat.
That's the pleasure, it seems to me, of writing."

—Stanley Elkin, as excerpted from
Conversations on Writing Fiction
by Alexander Neubauer

We dedicate this issue to hats.

Susan Burmeister-Brown
Linda Davies

CONTENTS

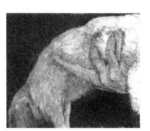

$\mathcal{C}$ONTENTS

Anxiously awaiting the next issue!
160

Steve Adams

This picture was taken at my grandparents' home outside of Conway, Arkansas. As a kid, I took great pride in being the first native-born Texan from either wing of the family. I don't know why, but I'm drawn to the way I'm holding the Oreo, as though there's some sort of clue there.

Four plays written by Steve Adams have been produced in New York City; he has also had plays produced or workshopped in Buffalo, Chicago, Los Angeles, and Austin, Texas. Adams is presently at work on his first novel. "The Fish," winner of Glimmer Train's New Writer Award, is his first published short story.

Adams lives in Austin, Texas.

STEVE ADAMS
The Fish

FIRST-PLACE WINNER
Short-Story Award
for New Writers

*C*ome daybreak, Ida knew what they'd find—Jake standing over one hundred twenty of his cattle he'd managed to pen and shoot, one by one. She knew full well that he'd lost his mind and she'd never have him back. She knew that she was now a widow.

Her porch light showed two cows that had escaped the pen standing in the black morning near the ranch house and looking out toward Jake's hissing kerosene lantern, the only other light for five miles. She clicked off her light and sat in her porch rocker.

She'd called the sheriff, but by the time he got there Jake was two-thirds finished and they couldn't see him in the dark and besides, as the sheriff said, "They're his cows anyway. No point in pushing a man into taking a shot at you." So he parked his patrol car up the dirt road and decided to wait for daylight.

A gunshot sounded from the pen and echoed off a mountain bluff a mile away. In the silence that followed, Ida heard the sheriff's radio crackle once, and then his voice calm and quiet, saying he'd presently be bringing Jake in. There was a garbled and mechanical reply, then the radio was turned off. The only indication of the sheriff in the darkness was the red pinpoint of his cigarette where he stood waiting outside his car. "He'll simmer down," he'd told her, "after he finishes."

But she knew there'd be no simmering down. It was the way Jake had said, "Good night, Ida," as he stepped out the screen door with his gun. On those words, whatever bond had held them together for forty-seven years snapped. And she saw Jake drifting into space like an astronaut who gets his cord to the mother ship cut in one of those sci-fi movies. She was on the mother ship. The mother ship was earth, and Jake was gone.

Her own calmness surprised her. But she'd known nights like this before. She'd been through the deathwatches of both her parents, and was there and awake when the trembling took her father and he opened his eyes, knowing what was coming. And she remembered when she was a girl and her neighbors, the Ramseys, lost their house to fire and had no insurance. Her mother gave their two little girls cookies and read them stories while the men dug through the ashes.

All her years had taught her that no matter how horrible the night, the next day the world would always be different; maybe not better, but changed and set off on a new course. And all you had to do was let the world take you that way. Her mother once told her that you can't let your heart break if no good can come of it.

With her toe, she pushed against the porch floor of the house and the rocker creaked back and forth. She knew the sun would be breaking through any moment to the east behind her. The fence had appeared in front of the house like a shadow, and a shrub or two on the other side of it were dark blurs. Each morning from the porch she watched the first light come up from the ground across the ranch like mist, objects crystallizing before her. Now she could see three tumbleweeds pressed against the fence and remembered the tumbleweed snowmen she had made each Christmas since she got the idea thirty years ago.

She leaned back in her chair and thought of Florida and her sister and realized that that was more than likely where she was headed. Good, she thought. Someplace different. Her sister had warned her against marrying Jake, said any man that would try and raise milk cows instead of beef cows in west Texas was crazy. "Jake's interested in milk," she'd heard herself say and regretted it the instant she said it. No way her sister was going to understand. Ida didn't understand herself, but she knew whatever made Jake want to raise milk cows against all common sense was tied in with the thing that made her love him.

To everyone's surprise, Jake somehow managed to turn a profit from his little dairy. The milk cows certainly weren't made for long-range, west Texas grazing, but he was able to cut a couple of good deals with local farmers for feed, and by irrigating was able to raise a few acres of alfalfa himself. And he sure didn't have to worry about competition for his milk.

Only when they first married did he say anything about the

STEVE ADAMS

cows. He explained that he just liked the idea of feeding babies, of them going from their mother's breast to him and his cows, then growing up and into the world. He liked being a part of that.

Ida wondered how many gentle and fragile people lived full, happy lives because the one event that could have pushed them over the edge never occurred. For Jake, that event was the test the people from Texas A&M ran on his milk. It showed traces of lead and arsenic, just within legal limits, and more than likely on the rise. What Jake could not get from his mind for the next three days was the thought that babies had been drinking his milk. Today was the fourth day.

Some young people had approached them about it, pointing fingers toward groundwater pollution and a toxic dump site. They wanted them to take it to court. But for those three days after the test it was all Ida could do to take care of Jake, and now it was too late to matter. With Jake gone, she was surprised how easily everything fell from her shoulders, how easily she could let go of the burden of this beautiful, desolate land. This was Jake's country, and she could not bear witness to it without him. And without Jake, it lost its claim on her. It would be easy enough to leave this house.

She remembered driving down the dirt driveway that Friday afternoon that the doctor told them that Jake couldn't father any children. She hated the doctor for that. He should've never said whose fault it was because it didn't matter. *They* couldn't have children, not Jake alone. Driving home he didn't say a word, and in the silence she became gripped by the fear he'd leave her. She knew he was thinking that he wasn't good enough for her, wasn't enough of a man. In bed that night she insisted he love her. Demanded it. And when he couldn't, and the coldness and distance swept into her, some dark part of herself opened and she did something she never thought she could do, then things she'd never even heard of. She was so shameless it scared him, but it woke him up and brought him to her. "It's not for babies," she told him. "It's for me. It's so you can please me."

A shot rang out, and she blushed, having been caught remembering *that,* then slowly began pushing those memories away. They didn't go easily. They seemed to flutter inside her like birds, frightened, insistent, white. She imagined opening a window and setting them free; watched them fly over the desert until the curves of their wings shrunk to pinpoints, then disappeared altogether into the sky.

There was nothing she could do to bring him back this time. She had nothing new to show him. He was through, and that was all. She knew him well enough to let him be.

"Accept, accept," she whispered as she slowly rocked. This part of her life was simply over. She told herself to count her blessings for forty-seven years with a man like Jake. And if her sister, Mae, brought it up, then Ida'd have to point out that her husband had only lasted twenty-five.

She thought again of Florida: she could get fresh seafood, and she remembered riding with Mae in the back seat of their Chevrolet the summer before the war when their folks took them to Galveston. Ida ordered flounder almost every meal. It infuriated Mae, who could see no point in eating a fish so silly it had both eyes on the same side of its face. But Ida explained that it simply wanted to see the sky. And Jake when he was courting her—she caught him lying on his back in a field in the middle of the morning. She walked out to him and asked him what he thought he was doing. "I reckon I'm just looking up," he told her. She watched him, then lay beside him. When he reached out and took her hand, she knew she was married.

Ida hadn't thought about the flounder since she was a little girl. She'd have to tell Mae, and Mae would tell her she was as crazy as Jake. Ida was surprised the thought could make her smile. It was daylight now, quiet, and she could see the sheriff ambling toward the pen.

SHORT-STORY AWARD FOR NEW WRITERS
1st- 2nd- and 3rd-Place Winners

➡ 1st place and $1200 to STEVE ADAMS, for "The Fish"

Adams' profile appears in this issue on page six, and his story begins on page seven.

➡ 2nd place and $500 to W. MICHAEL SINCLAIR, for "Sticky Valentines"

Born in 1956, Sinclair worked at a variety of service-industry jobs—janitor, barber, day-care worker—before entering a university in his thirties. He has since earned a B.S. in English at Washington University in St. Louis, and an M.F.A. from the University of Iowa.

Sinclair lives in Iowa City with Norma Sinclair and their children, Andy and Grace. He is currently tinkering with *Blind Date*, a manuscript of poetry; and an untitled collection of short fiction, which includes "Sticky Valentines."

W. Michael Sinclair
"Sticky Valentines"

For a minute the wind blew with the current. It split through Rodell's hair
at his temple. His eyes fell closed and he smiled. His entire face smiled,
creased and glowing in the river wind.

➡ 3rd place and $300 to DAWN DIEZ WILLIS, for "Mining Town"

A poet and writing teacher, Willis received her B.A. in Liberal Studies from San Diego State. Her poems have appeared in the *Southern Poetry Review*, the *Beloit Poetry Journal*, ZYZZYVA, and the *Berkeley Poetry Review*. She was the recipient of the Jessamyn West Award for Poetry in 1992 and a Vallecitos Residency Scholarship in 1994, and had a featured reading in the Valley Contemporary Poets series.

Willis lives in Salem, Oregon, and teaches poetry through the Arts in the Schools program.

Dawn Diez Willis
"Mining Town"

Takes all day to soap and scrub and rinse, and I only do it twice a month.
The rest of the month I live in a haze of human smells and grit, stains
blooming quietly on the clothes, towels, bedsheets like ghostly flowers. But
for that one day, with the sheets hung up in the wind and my underclothes
fresh and wet, my home smells so clean, almost like no smell at all.

We thank all entrants for sending in their work,
the reading of which was a delight and an honor for us.

PAUL THEROUX
Novelist as shapeshifter

Interview

by Michael Upchurch

While some readers know him best as a travel writer (The
Great Railway Bazaar, The
Happy Isles of Oceania), *Paul
Theroux started out as a fiction
writer in the late 1960s and still
thinks of himself primarily as a
novelist. His fiction embraces an
astonishing range of mood and
subject matter, with each new book
revealing yet another facet of his
vigorous and varied imagination.
Futuristic fantasy, hefty bildungs-
roman, sly postcolonial satire, sin-
ister psychosexual parable—
Theroux has done them all, al-
ways with a flourish distinctively his own.*

photo credit Ulf Andersen

Paul Theroux

His latest novel, Millroy the Magician, *finds him returning to a
U.S. setting with a tale about a vegetarian magician who starts his own
religion. Earlier novels evoke places where Theroux has lived or visited:
Malawi in* Jungle Lovers, *Singapore in* Saint Jack, *London in* The
Family Arsenal, *and Honduras in his best-known novel,* The
Mosquito Coast. *His upcoming projects include a collection of
"imaginary memoirs," one of which, "Lady Max," describes his
writing life in London during the time he was working on* The
Mosquito Coast.

Interview: PAUL THEROUX

Born in Medford, Massachusetts, in 1941, Theroux recently returned to the States after close to twenty years of living in London. He now divides his time between Cape Cod and Hawaii. In person, he has a quiet manner that occasionally gives way to passionate outburst. He was happy to talk about his itinerant life and his working methods, at one point holding up the pocket notebook he carries everywhere with him and saying, "This is a disk—an old-fashioned floppy disk. Very old-fashioned." But while his tools may be old-fashioned, the mind he brings to his chosen subject matter is always fresh.

UPCHURCH: *You left the States in 1963, when you were twenty-two years old. Was fiction on your mind at all when you left?*
THEROUX: Not at all. What I most wanted to do was leave—just get away as far as possible from the States.
Why?
I felt a sense of oppression and failure. I felt that the longer I stayed around, the more people would notice what I wasn't doing. I wasn't going to graduate school. I wasn't making any money. I didn't have any job prospects. I just wanted to get away and not be noticed. I also saw myself as someone who was able to go to a difficult or remote place and survive. More than survive: maybe prevail over it and have a good time.

I had a fantasy in which I saw myself, I think, as a kind of alienated stranger, an existential hero in an underdeveloped country, in a jungle and coping with it, perhaps even enjoying it, perhaps even staying there for a very long time, maybe for the rest of my life. I didn't approve of so many of the things that were going on in the States. The racism, the violence of the early sixties really just depressed me. And my own career seemed to be nonexistent.

So I was happy to go. But I wanted to go to a place where no one would follow me, no one would know me. I went to Italy first—and then I was going to go to Turkey. Turkey struck me as being a good place. Turkey was as far as I dared think about—

14   *Glimmer Train Stories*

Turkey, Lebanon, the Middle East. When the Peace Corps offered me the chance to go to central Africa, Nyasaland, I was thrilled because when I found out where it was I thought, "That's perfect." I couldn't *imagine* what life was like there. Put your finger right in the middle of Africa: that is Malawi. It was called Nyasaland then.

So I went there, and soon after that the Vietnam War got started and I was glad to be in Malawi. I was so far off I wasn't even part of the debate of whether we should be in Vietnam or not. I felt not. But I felt that some kind of alternative service was required if you objected. Not running away, and not saying, "No, I'm not going to join—I'm going to live my life." We were all aware in the Peace Corps that we were doing something useful, that we weren't just turning our backs on the draft.

When did it begin to dawn on you that this was something you could write about, something that would go in a novel?

I had always written about myself, my life, my experience, the things that I thought. It wasn't a dawning sensation. I knew that wherever I went I would be writing something. I never stopped writing. As a matter of fact, I wrote even when I was a premed student in college. I was writing short stories and poems, and starting novels and abandoning them.

When I was in Italy the summer after I graduated, I was writing. When I was in Peace Corps training, I kept a very detailed diary of what was happening, because it was such an odd thing. It was in Puerto Rico. We were there for a couple of months for Outward Bound training. I remember keeping up this diary, this running account of the camping, the rock climbing, and the relationships.

Once in a while in my life, in my early life especially, I ran across people who knew that I was writing, and they would express surprise. For example, in August in 1963, I was in Fano, Italy, on the Adriatic coast near Urbino, where I had a job. I was standing on the beach there—I remember the day; I remember the *time* of day—and I was talking to a college professor that I'd had. He taught the nineteenth-century English novel.

He was there visiting another college professor and he said, "What are you doing, Paul?"

And I said, "Oh, I'm here just having a good time."

He said, "How do you spend the day?"

I said: "I'm writing."

He said, "You're not!"

And I said, "What's wrong? What's wrong?" I started to get a little anxious, annoyed.

And he said, "It's just that I see you in that room staring at a blank page, with these beautiful blue skies, all this lovely country. Lovely blue skies and sunshine outside, and you're sitting in a room staring at a blank sheet of paper. I find that so sad."

Well, if I'd had a very big stick, I would have hit him over the head with it. I actually thought to myself: You son of a bitch. But I said, "Oh, well, I'm working on something."

His image of me was: This is a deluded dreamer.

An English professor! In other words: "Here you are in Italy. It's a sunny day. Why aren't you out—" God knows what I'd be doing. "Why aren't you out swimming?" I suppose he was threatened by the thought that I was inside in an Italian summer, working on something. And he imagined that I was looking at a blank piece of paper. And it wasn't a blank piece of paper! It was a very, very long poem. Now maybe it's lost to history. That doesn't matter. The thing is he didn't realize that that was my life, that that was something I enjoyed doing. That was the source of all my vitality. And he was contemptuous of it and sort of pitying me. That was the last time I saw him, but if I ever saw him again, I would bring it up and I'd say, "Do you remember what you told me?"

His name was Harold McCarthy. You might come across his name as the author of some pathetic little article. I'm sure he's dead or in some home for aged, clapped-out professors. But isn't that interesting? That was thirty-one years ago and I can remember it as if it was yesterday. Because I remember the feeling of: All my life I've tried to get away from people who have dismissed the idea of writing; I go to Italy to write and I run into this guy who's a college professor, and he's disdainful.

So that was another of the reasons I went away. That attitude. That was a very prevalent attitude: People saying what are you doing; why are you doing it; how are you going to make any money; how are you going to support a family? What he was saying more or less was: "You're wasting your time." Well, everyone knows you're not wasting it! This is a craft; this is an *art*. This is something you have to work at. Would he have said that if I was sketching pictures? You can see that even now it's making me cross.

A lot of writers leave home in order to write about home. But straight off, in the early novels, you weren't writing about Medford; you were writing about your new home. It seems an odd decision for a young writer to make.

That's perhaps true. But I wasn't able to write about home until I wrote *My Secret History*. I really couldn't address myself to home in fiction for about twenty-five years. It wasn't that I lacked perspective. I just didn't know what there was to write about. I couldn't somehow see what the subject was. First I couldn't write about it because I didn't want to write about myself. I didn't want to write about even someone who resembles me. And I couldn't use it.

The fact is that I felt I had no status at home, growing up. I felt that I was nobody and that I was nowhere. People say, "Oh, you come from Boston. How wonderful. They're more English than the English." I felt, coming from Boston, that I didn't come from anywhere. I thought I just came from a neighborhood, and I think it's true—that I did just come from a neighborhood. But all the comedy that I grew up with—the ethnic comedy, the ethnic jokes, the Italians, the Irish—it didn't occur to me that that was a good subject until much later. And it was a territory that I was very much an outsider in. I wasn't Italian and I wasn't Irish. Those were the two ethnic groups that mattered. So people who come from that background had a place in it and could write about it. I don't know whether there's a big Italian novel set in Boston, but there should be one because it's a very, very funny society.

When I was in Africa, I didn't see Boston. I had turned my back so squarely on it, I didn't *want* to see it. I wasn't interested in it, and I thought: "I'm not going to write about it." What I wanted to write about was a simpler, more immediate situation, which was Africa.

What was the publishing climate like for a young American trying to sell books about postcolonial Africa? It must have seemed a long shot.

Maybe. Maybe not. Maybe it was an advantage to be this solitary figure so far away, so isolated-looking that it made me conspicuous and more interesting. Maybe it would have been more difficult if I had been in Boston, Massachusetts, where the publisher was: Houghton Mifflin. I think that perhaps it was an advantage. I don't know. The writing might have helped. I think *Fong and the Indians* is a pretty good book. *Girls at Play* is a good book. *Jungle Lovers*, certainly.

They hold up well.

I hope so. I haven't reread them—I don't know. But there were more books being published then. I know this to be a fact. In the sixties, all publishers—Houghton Mifflin, Putnam, William Morrow, Knopf—published more books than they do now. They published more books that sold a small number of copies. Having a sale of five thousand wasn't a disgrace. Ten thousand was fairly respectable. Fifteen thousand? Good. Twenty thousand? Great! Nowadays, if you sell five thousand, they'll tell you that they're not interested.

I wasn't making much money out of it. My advances were

18

really small. But I wasn't in it for the money. I was in it for life. It was my career and my life. And I thought: "I simply want to go on publishing—and if I can make a living at it, so much the better."

I knew that I would always be able to make a living one way or another, writing something, because I felt that I had the ability to write anything: essays, travel, short stories, novels. I thought that I could stick at it and simply by working very hard I could do it. I see this quality in a lot of people today. My kids, for example. I know their attitude: "All I have to do is work hard." My kids have that attitude because they saw me just sitting at my desk for so many years.

The early novels were written in very immediate reaction to the place where you were at the time. At some point you began to write books set in places far away from where you were: The Mosquito Coast *was written in London and I gather "Lady Max" was written in the South Pacific.*

All over the place.

Was there some change of gear, in your mind or approach?

Not a change of gear, but I wrote with a great intensity in the 1960s and early seventies. I was writing about what was immediate. I was trying to give some kind of fictional expression to events I witnessed, and I was very responsive to events. You have to remember that I was publishing a lot, that this wasn't just one book germinating over a long period.

To choose an example, I went to Singapore and I was forbidden to write. I had signed a contract with the Singapore authorities as a condition of teaching at the University of Singapore. They said, "You can't write or publish anything while you're here."

And I said, "Well, I won't publish anything, but no one's going to stop me from writing."

So the whole time I was in Singapore I was working on the *Sinning with Annie* stories and *Jungle Lovers*. I also wrote my book about V.S. Naipaul there. So in the three years, I wrote three books—and published them soon after I left. But as soon as I finished *Jungle Lovers*, while I was still in Singapore, I started *Saint Jack*. So I was responding to my being in Singapore.

I felt over the hill in Singapore. I felt very burdened. I was married with two children. I had a very poorly paying job. I was terribly overworked. It was very hot. I had no money. And I felt like a failure. I felt old. I felt fifty. I thought fifty was old because the oldest people I knew there were fifty. And they were bitter. "Fucked up and far from home" summed up my feeling and their feeling. So *Saint Jack* is about that. That's something I probably wouldn't do now, but at the time I was processing information very fast.

Do you have a person who acts as a sounding board for your writing? In "Lady Max," in the memoirlike element of the story, you read chapters from a book that resembles The Mosquito Coast *aloud to your wife, Anne. Is that usual with you?*

At that time, from *Girls at Play* to a little beyond *The Mosquito Coast*, so from the mid-sixties to the early eighties, I used to read to my wife—my then wife. And it was a sounding board; it was something to do in the evening. It was a pleasant experience of just sitting down, having a drink, with something I'd done during the day. Or I'd do it maybe every few days, when I'd finished a chapter.

And whenever I finished, she'd say, "Go on—then what?"

And I'd say, "No, that's as far as I've got."

She'd say, "Oh ... I like that. But I'm not too sure about your description of this." Or: "Should he have said this or done that?"

It was a lovely experience. To me, it was one of the most pleasant experiences of my life, reading to her. And I was reading to her because I hadn't seen her all day—she was at work—because I needed encouragement, and because I needed her critical gift. That was very important to me, all of that. And, you see, I worked every weekday, and had something to read to her.

And then— It didn't stop, because my wife used to read manuscripts after that. She read "Doctor Slaughter" [collected in *Half Moon Street*] and responded to that. Then *The Kingdom by the Sea*, she read that in typescript. All of them she read in typescript. But the daily reading tapered off.

I put in "Lady Max" all the happy moments: my London happiness. That's a story about writing in London, for anyone who's wondered what the writer's life was like in London if you were of that age. It was set around 1978-79. How old was I then? Thirty-six, thirty-seven. I don't know if that's old or young. I felt very much on top of things in some respects. In other respects, I was sort of living on Grub Street. Jonathan Raban was part of that life. Martin Amis was just a little guy working as an assistant at the *New Statesman*, and I used to see him every so often. And then there were more grand figures around, like Angus Wilson, V.S. Pritchett, Anthony Burgess.

So I deliberately wrote that story to encapsulate that wonderful experience—the experience of living in London, writing during the day, the winter. I always loved writing in the winter when it was dark. "Writing weather," I used to think. "Writing light." It was dark, with just a pool of artificial light. Everyone indoors. I was indoors, working on something good. And there was a completeness to it and a monotony to it that I needed.

But I stopped having a sounding board in the mid- to late eighties, I guess. My wife read my manuscripts, but I think I became more isolated. I haven't really thought too much about this until you asked me the question—but I stopped having an editor and stopped having, pretty much, a sounding board. I guess by then I was so busy and so isolated that I was simply writing. I was writing and then sending it to the publisher. My wife read the books, but not in a critical sense. I was looking for her approval, of course, but she didn't suggest many changes.

What's your center of publication? Do things come out in Britain first, and is Britain where you work more closely with an editor?

No, I don't have an editor and I haven't had one since my editor at Houghton Mifflin, Joyce Hartman, retired in the early eighties.

What was the last book she worked on?

I have a feeling it might have been *The Mosquito Coast*. But it also might have been *The Old Patagonian Express* or the book of short stories, *World's End*, that I dedicated to her. Since then, I've had a lot of people who were nominally my editors, but they didn't do any editing. The whole process of editing for me, and I think for a lot of people, ended around that time, when editors began to be people that got authors for publishers, the ones who persuaded authors to leave whatever publishing house they were with and join other publishing houses for more money. And then, really, you didn't hear from them.

I had various people at Houghton Mifflin. Robie Macauley, for example, was my editor. I never got a phone call from him. I don't ever remember getting a letter from him. Every so often, I would see him and he would say something. But he didn't do any editing. And he was the editor—nominally the editor.

An editor, to me, is someone who stays in touch, has an influence, is your protector, writes you long, interesting letters, and when you call up, they answer the phone, and if you say, "Can you do this?" they do it. And they then say to you, "The manuscript is good, but there are things that we have to look at." Then they go through the manuscript and they say, "This word, that word—" Or maybe: "This chapter's a bit too long—" Whatever. They edit. They make suggestions. Sometimes you take the suggestions, sometimes not. That hasn't happened after Joyce Hartman. She was not an "important" person in the publishing house and I think that she never realized how good she was. She was Jewish and a bit like a Jewish mother or an auntie. But she was just the person I needed.

At some point, letter writing became telephoning. And now faxing and telephoning are the way. The whole epistolary relationship between author and editor has ended. I'm not talking about a literary letter. I'm just talking about a friendly letter, a correspondence. I miss that. When I wasn't making a lot of money, this sort of charm, friendship, love, and attention took the place of money. I didn't need money. I didn't even notice that I wasn't making money. And then when I drove a harder bargain, I became someone who, I think, looked as though he didn't need charm, attention, affection, and love. And I became, if not an employee, at least someone who was then paid off by the publisher. And I had no ally.

In essays and interviews, you've talked about your writing habits: writing in longhand, planning only a few chapters ahead of time. You also express surprise at Joyce Cary's practice of writing the climactic scene of a novel first and then building the book around it. I can see that in a book like The Mosquito Coast *there's an improvisatory genius at work a little like that of Allie Fox, the hero, who makes it up as he goes along when he and his family abandon the United States for the wilds of Central America. But in reading* The Family Arsenal, *the plot (about terrorist activities in London) seems so intricately pieced together that it's hard for me to imagine that you didn't have much of it planned out ahead of time.*

Actually, *The Mosquito Coast* was very carefully planned out. All of them were. But if you plan a book too much, then the element of discovery and surprise, which all writing should offer, doesn't occur. So it's wrong to have it so heavily plotted that you're not open to the serendipity of the creative spark, where something just occurs to you. You begin writing, and your characters are speaking, and then they seem to take on a life of their own. That should happen in all books. But I've never really started a book without knowing where I was going.

With *The Mosquito Coast*, I had it plotted to the end. The only thing was, I thought that the last part of it was going to be much longer. Then when Allie died, I thought: "There's no plot; that's the end of the story; he's the only person that matters here, and he's gone. I can't push this further." The last part, called "The Mosquito Coast"—it's very short—looks the way it does as a little memorial to the way it was going to be.

That was going to be a very long section where the family just went from pillar to post. They built a boat; the boat was destroyed; they were navigating along the coast; they met hostile people; they got sick. It was going to be a chapter of accidents, about fifty or a hundred pages long.

But I saw that that wasn't possible, that that couldn't happen. I started writing that, and it didn't work—there was no Allie in it.

When you started, did you know Allie would be silenced by vultures plucking out his tongue? Or was that one of the imaginative discoveries?

That was one of the discoveries. I knew he was going to die, and I knew at what point in the book he was going to die. I just wasn't quite sure how it was going to happen—whether he was going to die from a bullet, whether it was going to be an accident, or whether his kids were going to kill him. At one time, I thought his kids were going to kill him. Then thinking about it, when I got nearer to it, worked up to it, I saw that that wasn't going to happen. They can't do it. They should do it—but if they do it, they're going to be marked by it.

That was just an interesting technical problem. I knew what the sequence was going to be. What I have trouble with is how long it's going to take to develop a sequence. I knew, for example, that the beginning of *The Mosquito Coast* was going to be this asparagus farm in Massachusetts. I thought it might be a chapter or two. Well, it turned out to be quite a bit longer than that. I can't remember how long—but a lot.

The first part of *Millroy the Magician*, similarly, I thought the county fair was going to be one chapter—the fair, and then Jilly [the book's teenage narrator] disappears and ends up in Millroy's trailer, and off they go: the book begins. But, actually, the county fair occupies much more space because, in elaborating the characters and the situation, it usually takes more space than I envisage. I'm very, very bad at imagining the size of a book— pretty good at plotting, pretty good at characterization, I think. It's just that I never know about length. I start a short story and it sometimes becomes a novella. Sometimes it's just a three-page story.

With a novel, I know it's going to be a novel. I just don't know how long of a novel it's going to be. And so *Millroy* is a bit longer than I intended to write. And *The Mosquito Coast* is about the length that I was looking for, but I thought there was going to be, as I say, the section at the end. I can't think of any other instances where that's the case. But I'm always surprised by the length of time that it takes me to write—always much longer than I expect.

You have a talent for languages and a good ear for dialect. Does your knowledge of other languages affect your style in English—images, word choice, phrasing? And are you drawn to one vernacular over another?

I'm very interested in speech patterns. Does the knowledge of another language help with that? Perhaps it does. I think, though, that it's part of the same thing: If you have an ear for languages, then you have an ear for the way people speak, whether they're speaking in another language or in their own idiolect, or slang, or regional accent. I find that it's a tremendous source of comedy, the way people speak, and of characterization. No one speaks the same. No one has the same speech patterns. So if you can catch the speech patterns of a person, you're a long way toward describing the person. I always thought it was one of my strengths: writing dialogue.

Is there a connecting thread that you're aware of in your work? In writing Millroy, *did you ever stop and say, "Oh, I've done this before, but from another angle, and here we go again with this particular obsession"?*

I think so. Here's what I think is a connecting thread—or not a connecting thread, but a situation I seem to write about a lot:

a man taking up with a rather innocent woman, a girl often, or a person taking up with a person who's innocent. I don't seem to have equal relationships. I don't seem to have Strong Man/ Strong Woman.

Why do I do that? Because *I* haven't had relationships like that. Why, I wonder, do I return to that a lot? I think I write about it from all the different points of view, but certainly the old person and the young person, the master/student, the Svengali/ Trilby figure, is something that I have returned to again and again.

Another thing that I return to a lot is a fear of death—not always as death but as extinction—because obviously it must upset me.

There's another thing: the idea of a person in a highly colored background, or the person in the foreground is highly colored. In other words, a tremendous contrast, whether it's a cultural contrast or whatever: a Chinese person in Africa, an American in Singapore.

All of that strikes me as being characteristic of motifs, I'd say, more than themes that I've pursued. Even the way a person speaks. When you take a person speaking in an unusual way, that's set against paragraphs of considered prose and you have some kind of stark or unusual contrast, maybe just of color, but it's something that fascinates me, as though in a hotel lobby you had a Tibetan monk sitting in a chair, sipping tea. That's something that I would find wonderful: a man in saffron robes in a very unlikely setting. And I suppose it's the comedy implicit in it—and the reality implicit in it. The fact that a lot of life is like that: it's not just everybody in a pinstripe suit.

I think probably sex—either implied or stated—has been quite a common feature in a lot of my work. Whether that was written out of sexual frustration or just a highly sexed nature that I have, or had, I don't know. You can read and read other people's books and not find it—just find, you know, fairly straightforward business. Whereas the unusual has always interested me. There's an element of wish-fulfillment in all the books, something vicarious. I often have written a book instead of doing the deed. I always fantasized about taking my family to a little jungle clearing and being a sort of Swiss Family Robinson family. I often fantasized *The Mosquito Coast* like that. Jack Flowers in *Saint Jack* says, "Fiction seemed to give me the second chances life denied me," but I think sometimes it's not even a second chance—you can fulfill your fantasies in some writing.

Those are just some of the things that occur to me. But I can't be my own reader. It's one of the unfortunate things. You can't sit down and enjoy the meal that you just cooked. You serve it to someone else who often has quite a different reaction because they're reading in a day or two what it took you a year or two to write.

I've always enjoyed your use of exclamation marks. And in rereading Saint Jack, *I noticed that in the book's opening paragraph there's a comment about "the soul of the writer flapping on the clothespin of his exclamation mark." What is your philosophy of exclamation marks, or do you have one?*

In punctuation, generally, I don't use a lot of semicolons. I tend to use colons rather than semicolons. Dashes—I've exploited the dash quite a lot. The exclamation mark I've used, I hope, to good advantage. All of these are things that it's very easy to overdo. A question in the middle of a paragraph is something I've found is a way of sending or turning a paragraph or an issue around. A question mark in expository prose is often a wonderful thing. Too many questions, and you're done for. Too many exclamation marks, and you're done for. It's all a matter of balance and proportion, I guess.

When I wrote *The Mosquito Coast*, I was trying to write not so much the way a thirteen-year-old would speak—because we all know thirteen-year-olds may or may not have that vocabulary—but to have a thirteen-year-old's rhythm. When that book went to the copy editor, they took out almost every dash and turned it into a semicolon. I started to rub them out, and then I gave it back and said, "Please, put all my punctuation back. It was all done deliberately." The same thing with *Millroy*. So I think it's more the dash than the exclamation mark. But I find judicious use of punctuation to be very effective. I hate prose that's overpunctuated. And I've always tried to write with the utmost clarity of expression, but without simplifying.

You have some awfully unusual names in your books—Parker Jagoda in Chicago Loop, *Orlo Fedewa and Mister Phyllis in* Millroy, *and many others. Do you keep a names notebook?*

Every so often I do, or a name occurs to me. I have been known to make long lists of names. In all the notebooks, the working notebooks for novels, I have pages of names. I read obituaries just for the names. I was very glad and felt vindicated when I saw that Henry James did that—and I'm no Henry James, we know that. But Henry James's notebooks push on for a couple of pages, then you see long lists of very funny names, always terrific names, and he got them from the *Times* obituaries. Nothing's worse than having a character and thinking: "I had a name—I just can't think of it."

In Picture Palace *your narrator, photographer Maude Coffin Pratt, says, "Subject is everything. Technique is only something to conceal." How close is that to your philosophy?*

I think your technique shouldn't be obvious. I was reading *Absalom, Absalom!* the other day, and I was thinking how obvious and deliberate Faulkner's style is. It's this wonderful story, but it's not well told. That will probably annoy all the Faulkner scholars. But I think there's something deeply wrong with that book and with Faulkner's style. I can see that it's him, but it needs a little work. That sounds like an awful thing to say. But I would say some of Hemingway needs a little work. And I'm not saying that it doesn't express them. It does—I can see how it expresses them. But I found *Absalom, Absalom!* unreadable for its obvious technique.

Is that something that's changed? Because, if you're now rereading the book, you must have read it with pleasure the first time.

Not a lot of pleasure. I read it as a book that we studied—that's the trouble. And I didn't read it with enough of my critical faculties. I feel the same way about a lot of things, about painting where you see the technique. A lot of it is simply decorative; it's just like interior decoration. It's not something I enjoy looking at. So figurative painting is really the only kind that I'm actually attracted to. That seems a philistine thing to say, but in abstract art, all I see is technique: I don't see any ideas in it.

In writing, excessive use of italics can be very off-putting— or too many narrators, stories within stories, eccentric para-graphing or absence of punctuation. All of those things. So what do we do about *Finnegans Wake*? I don't know *what* we do about *Finnegans Wake*! Except just stand four paces away and admire it—but don't imitate it. *Ulysses* is a masterpiece, no question. It has excessive technique, but it actually works. It sounds a bit pompous that I should be approving of Joyce, giving Joyce the nod. But that's an example of lots of technique. You have to be a genius to get away with that, and there aren't enough geniuses around to do it. The rest of us have to depend on something much simpler: being ourselves, rather than assuming elaborate techniques that we haven't mastered.

What's the biggest difference between travel writing and fiction?

Simply that with a travel book you are, or ought to be, faced with recording a trip which you've taken. You know it has a beginning, a middle, and an end, and you know *how* it ends. You know every detail of the journey. A novel is a work of the imagination largely, and depends on the daily discovery of things happening. You know pretty much what your route is, but you don't know everything that's lying along that route. And so the element of imagination in a novel is crucial.

It can be the death of a travel book, taking liberties. I always saw myself as a novelist. Even when I was in Africa for almost six years, I never saw myself writing a travel book, recording a journey that I had taken. I always saw myself as transforming my experience into fiction.

I took lots of trips. I went into the Congo; I went to Nigeria. I took trips up to Tanzania, to Uganda, lived in the bush, worked in a leper colony, took long rides, sometimes was away for a month or two. I never saw myself hurrying back and writing an account of that. I always saw it as a comedy of Indians, Africans, and whites trying to live together and failing at it. And I will say, apropos of that, that I did not begin to write well until I saw that life is essentially comedy and farce.

Whenever I've tried to write solemnly about a situation, I've failed. I can only write about it from a comic perspective. I'm not saying comedy's not serious—I think it is—but I wasn't able to write about Africa until I could conceive of it as comedy.

What are the best conditions for writing?

The monotony of staying in one place is the best thing for writing a novel. Having regular habits, a kind of security, but especially no big surprises, no shocks—for me, I'm talking about. Just to be in a room, plugging away. That's the best thing for you. Personal appearances, prizes—all those are disruptions. You need encouragement; you need good things to happen to you, cheerful people around you. But I have never been able to work well except in a very monotonous, predictable atmosphere, with placid, even-tempered people. I can't be around excitable people.

In Saint Jack, *Jack Flowers says, "Fifty-three is a convenient age for a tycoon." Now that you've reached that age, are you, in the literary scheme of things, a tycoon? And is this a convenient age to be one?*

Being fifty was quite a big thing for me. As you get older, you keep revising your idea of what old age is. When I wrote *The Black House*, the main character, Alfred Munday, was forty. And I thought forty was pretty old. Jack Flowers is fifty—that's over the hill. Now, I don't know. I don't think anyone's old who doesn't feel old.

You now have the success that Jack Flowers coveted at fifty.

Or that I wanted then. Is it convenient? If material success had come to me early, I don't know what would have happened. I will say that, at the time, I hated being indigent. I hated having to write for money.

You say, "Is it convenient?" Yeah, I wouldn't want to have a financial problem now. And yet, if I had one, I could think of lots of ways of solving it. I set out to be a writer and to write, and I had a certain image of what was expected of a writer and what rewards I could get. I never had the idea that I would become prosperous, but I always knew that I would be able to go on writing.

Every good thing that has happened to me has been a surprise. It's never been something that I expected or demanded. It was always a bonus of writing. Publishing books early on and getting advances for only one or two thousand dollars—it didn't matter to me. Of course I would have wanted more. But that didn't discourage me. It didn't make me say, as it does some people, "I'm not going to sweat my guts out for a pittance."

I was perfectly willing to sweat my guts out for a pittance because I had the book. I always felt that the book was the thing, that if a book was any good, it had a long and fruitful life. So I wasn't looking for a killing, and I despise people who boast about large advances. I had a family. I educated my children, and I never had, I guess, a serious money worry. I don't know what would have happened if I had made a killing early on. I honestly don't think it would have changed anything.

I wouldn't have had as interesting a life, though. That's for sure.

MICHAEL UPCHURCH is a Seattle writer whose novels include *Air* and *The Flame Forest.*

William Luvaas

*My first attempts at writing were in peanut butter on
the kitchen walls. Sadly, in time, I was expected to give
that up.*

William Luvaas's first novel, *The Seductions of Natalie Bach,* was published by
Little, Brown. His new novel, *Going Under,* is forthcoming from Putnam
(September 1994). His stories have appeared in many publications, including
Confrontation, Short Story, and the *Village Voice.* His story "The Firewood
Wars" was co-winner of *Fiction Network*'s National Fiction Competition in
1986.

Luvaas lives in San Marcos, California, with his wife, Lucinda, a visual artist.

WILLIAM LUVAAS
Yesterday after the Storm

*W*e were looking for parts of the house that had been severed, my boy Jeffrey and me. Cut right off or crushed outright like some devil-knows-what fist whumped it flat. It was hysteria: the wind gasping rumors about children who bobbed down-stream in the potty their mama set them upon just before it began. I picture them standing bolt upright in their leavings, gripping ceramic rims and twirling 'round like the octopus ride at the county fair. Myrna Haney observed two of the diapered sea captains bobbing over muddy rapids in her backyard, bawling back to their tonsils, arriving—so Myrna claims—sixty miles south, waterlogged, so hoarse their jaw hinges stuck open and wouldn't close. I'm talking toddlers here—three, four years old. Mighty traumatic at that age to see your mama swept along with you out the window when the yellow flood burst through the bathroom door, clinging to the toilet seat for dear life until her arms give out, then ducking under. Like I said, rumors. The wind curls them off whitecaps and sloshes them like mud patties against consciousness. I cannot recall there being a lake in Sterner County, let alone the sea now stretching from the edge of my property on into infinity.

Rumors, too, about the two Lilies: my wife and daughter. "Seen 'em sitting side by side at Jabberwocky down to Hempsberg slushing whiskey sours. Both of 'em, big and little, look-alikes sitting side by side. Lushed," old Towers tells me, but the man has been known to talk just to hear words lisped together. Besides, big Lily don't drink. What she does or doesn't, Lily Junior does or doesn't. Just the same.

People mumble about Noah's ark. Two did this morning when Jeff and I stopped by Melinda's for breakfast. Couldn't very well breakfast at home with both Lily and the kitchen gone. I asked Melinda Haney, "How come you lasted and we was wiped out?"

"Faith," she said.

"Not a broken window," I marveled. "Why, the newspaper stands, still upright, outside."

"It come just so far then it stopped," said Henry Staidly. One of the regulars, Henry.

"Faith." Melinda poured Jeffrey coffee. My prostate has begun to just say no. "Tea, Lawrence?" she asked. "I have Oolong Loopsong and Constant Comment, all like that."

"Oolong is close," I said, "but I don't believe it's scripture, Melinda."

She sighed hard and spoke to Henry. "The difference between your believer and heathen is this, Henry: Believers do not fuss over split hairs. They are secure and sound in the truth."

"Meaning?" I asked.

"Meaning ye may judge him by the smallness in a man."

I nudged Jeffrey on the stool beside me (he reached my shoulder now, seemed pleased in that, but wasn't talking this morning). "What redeems the Haney sisters—if they can't find a verse to fit the occasion, they invent one. That's flexible Christianity. No, thanks just the same, Melinda. They say there's as much caffeine in a tea leaf as a coffee bean. You'll note back in history it wasn't until Marco Polo opened the tea routes that Europe became dangerous. All that caffeine."

"Understand you lost your house," said Henry.

"Western half."

"And Mum 'n' Lily," Jeff mumbled.

"Half your house and half the family," Melinda shook her head, leaning on arms that were rusted lampposts, splotched and freckled. "A righteous man does not build his house on sand. You have this upon your own head, Lawrence Connery."

"I don't want to hear that this morning, Melinda. Not with my Lilies missing."

"He don't seem all that upset about it, you ask me," said a rancher down the counter. "I lost half my herd. Can't bring myself to work this morning a'tall."

"I'm just about to get upset," I snapped.

"Aftershock," Henry Staidly nodded his large head. "There's people after Hiroshima walked in a daze for a week with skin hanging from their necks. Jap people, but all the same—"

"I don't want to hear that either, Henry. Jeff, I believe we will go. We would find better neighbors in Los Angeles."

That's when someone mentioned Noah's ark. Not Melinda but one of the kitchen help. Poor thing. Once they started talking biblical, you knew they would soon be out of a job. Melinda hired sinners; once she converted them, she fired the lot to hire new. Good Christianity, she claimed, and good capitalism. Allowed her to practice her faith seven days a week.

"D'you think my wife and little girl might be on that ark?"

"Don't tempt the Lord." Melinda wagged a finger thick and waxy as a dinner taper.

Henry Staidly tapped my arm, his eyes fixed on Jeff. "I wouldn't dig in the backyard, Lawry. Leave that to deputies."

I don't believe I'd ever looked at the man: eyes small and side-tilted, lips strung straight as barbed wire. Henry's hair had whitened, but moustache and eyebrows remained basic black; he seemed to be trying to make up his mind.

"I appreciate your concern, Henry, but I don't want to hear that either."

As we left, Melinda glanced heavenward; her lips moved. I kicked over newspaper stands outside, then shrugged at my son. "No newspapers anyway, long as I can remember."

"Do we have to look, Daddy?" he asked.

"No, sir. And we won't. When a storm reaches into your house and pulls your mom and sister into the air, you should be a little respectful. We'll wait and see."

Looking back

They say tornados will jump hill to hill, house to house; I suppose that's what it did. Taking mine and leaving Melinda's. Taking Milton Norge's, leaving the Lipsongs'. Midge Talmadge's barn sat across the road, back half of it. Pitchforks, scoop shovel, tack hung neatly against the back wall, but the hayloft had dislodged violently, joists compound-fractured from the frame, raw splinters jutting out. (The county cut a hole through for cars to pass like they do with redwoods out in California and left it there as a tourist attraction.) Midge herself lay somewhere. So did my girls, big and little Lily.

They had been in Lily Junior's bedroom reading to each other when the storm hit. The room was what we call a floater, perched on stilts beside the house. My intention was to build a garage beneath, but with inflation and life's pesterups, I never got to it. The twister got hold and tore it away clean before flattening the roof into the second story. Jeff was coming downstairs at the time, heard a sound, he says, like an adhesive bandage torn away from skin. If he hadn't jumped at that instant, he would have wound up in the basement beneath the upper story.

You can live a lot of time in a few thick seconds. First, that forewarning, an animal thing deep in sinuses, air crowded against eardrums, adenoids swelled like tiny helium balloons, then— well it had been raining a steady flush—rain stopped flat. I stood there looking out through the screen door, worried as hell

Sluggard's Creek would flood and form a new bed down Main Street and on through my front door, when a denser shadow loomed against seeming total blackness, swayed east, hip-wiggled over what must've been Sluggard's Hill (though I couldn't see it), leaped—yes, I saw that clearly, like a small boy leaps a shrub, stops to calibrate height then jumps in place—over Melinda's, and (already a thought half-formed in my mind: *Damned believers! With their luck, I'd be smug too*) then was atop us, pulling up a little swirling light as it come—dogs, pebbles, standing water, my hair, my shout TORNADO. My wife and daughter.

You have likely seen pictures of it: First mate lashed to the wheel while clothes snap on his body, torso pulses like a sail on taut nerves of the wind. It shouldn't be possible for him to remain, but he does. Until Jeffrey clipped me beneath the knees in his vacuumed rush from the house and we somersaulted shoe over seatpants down the front walk pursued by domestic furnishings. But the tornado had passed on with what it wanted. Women mainly this time. A harried, hungry, madly phallic God.

Later, I would dig house paint and slivers from beneath my fingernails and hate myself for not letting go. Then again, maybe in clinging I had saved my son's life.

We made a pile on the front porch, which was still roofed and standing—twisted chairs, dented pots, towels, bedroom slippers. Myrna Haney stopped by to place big Lily's red felt hunting hat atop the mound. "Found this on my rosebush," she said. "Well, I recognized it right off and walked 'round the house calling on the Lilies. They say you lost them. Lord deliver them up to mercy."

"They're missing." I glanced at Jeff—who attempted to dislodge his bicycle from a mud mound the color of salmon loaf—and held a finger to my lips. "Just missing."

Myrna tsk-tsked. "You don't know to cry or laugh. Like when Lazarus come back to the quick."

"I'm smiling, Myrna. I see you survived all right."

"Envy is a sin, Brother Lawrence."

"No, ma'am. Sad as I am, there's no room for envy."

Glancing down the ruined street, she turned a tortoise's pale eye and her outhouse breath upon me. "Why, what use would they have of me at my age? I will tell you something I have never told a soul, Lawry, because you are grieving and I have a mind to forgive your shamelessness." She whispered in a haunted tone, "A woman widowed long as I am can't eat her own cooking."

"Why don't you eat at the diner then?"

"Sixteen women and girls, all beneath the age of forty-five. Now you answer me that."

"I couldn't. I don't know your meaning."

Her eyes propped wide in amazement. "Well, I guess you don't see. It snatched the leaven from your loaf and you don't see."

"It opened some drawers, Myrna, took the linens. Others it left closed beside them. Had a special fondness for socks."

"Not one single boy," she eyed Jeff wolfishly.

He'd dug up the bicycle but only the rear wheel, and he was distraught about it. "First I lost my mum and sister, now my bike," he whimpered. "It ain't fair."

I put an arm around the boy. "Nothing fair about it. Or right. Or sensible. It takes what it wants and goes away, like a fat man at a snack counter."

Myrna leaned forward, cheek crinkled as a fennel leaf but abrasive as it brushed mine. "What the Lord whispers in the wind, Lawrence, I'll pluck it out."

"I trust you will, Myrna, and I appreciate it."

The Haney sisters, Myrna and Melinda, are baleen hereabout: sifting worthy rumors from useless, taking it upon themselves to spread them. "Gossip is the devil's work," Melinda explained one Friday night when we had taken into it, "but rumor is a blessing. Did you know the Book contains 146 rumors but not one gossip."

"Didn't know and don't believe it."

"'Rumor of war, rumor of rain, rumor of peace, rumor shall be upon rumor.' Ezekiel 7:26."

"'...And mischief upon mischief,'" I shot back (knowing that one). "Meaning rumor is a mischief."

"A mischief, Lawrence Connery, is a man who don't believe in the revealed word of God before his face. I swear, if you sat in the Holy Ghost's lap you'd ignore him and turn on television."

"Damn tootin'," I laughed, "and make sure he couldn't get at the remote."

Melinda pinched her lips: an obscene pink display like the inner flesh of a chrysanthemum or a schoolgirl kicking up her skirts, made more obscene by the manly squareness of her chin and eyes greasy from years in the kitchen. "Truth is truth, rumor is uncertain truth, and gossip is devious truth. Begin a rumor and the truth is sure to catch up."

"I've heard it rumored you were wild and lusty in your youth, Melinda. Took to strong drink and sexual promiscuity."

She flared; I thought she would slug me. Given her size, I'd have had a time of it. "A man who don't open his eyes don't know what he has seen. Why, you know very well I was a lesbian besides back then. Redeemed in the blood of the lamb."

"That's an awful image, Melinda. A plump lesbian soaked in lamb's blood."

She blustered. "You may call me 'fat' or 'dumpling cakes' or 'lard ass,' but if you are my friend, Lawrence, you will not call me plump. Adolescents, geese, and old dogs are plump."

"Sorry, Melinda, I didn't know you were sensitive on the subject."

By next morning

The water had subsided some, and I wished it hadn't; nothing but silt and trash left in its wake. Neighbors—what remained of them—stopped by with rumors. I suspected the Haney sisters were busy. Someone had met a mother and daughter who answered to "big and little" on the road to Haneysville, disheveled and dazed. A logger cut down a loblolly pine in a half-decimated forest up past Boone. When the tree crashed to earth, he found a girl clinging to its upper branches. Sadly, the tree had crushed her. A bathrobe matching big Lily's blue terry, a see-through nightie, and floppy ape's-foot slippers were found on a wooden Indian up at Trader Tom's in Traceyville. No sign of the woman who'd been wearing them, but could have been Lily. Trader Tom left the Indian in the getup, hoping to take an edge on the tourist trade.

Troubles me to think the storm would strip off a woman's clothes and toss her naked in midair. Too much like Myrna Haney's horror stories. Where do they end up, all these women? In fat sheiks' harems? Chained in basements in Hershey, Pennsylvania? On phone-sex lines in Los Angeles? They get them somewhere. Who can say anymore whether the powers that be serve good or evil. They say the CIA controls rain in Cuba and the Atomic Energy Commission controls earthquakes in California. Who regulates tornados?

Halfheartedly, Jeff and I repaired the roof. No sense driving around looking for the girls. From my place the tornado had headed due east to Midge Talmadge's barn, cutting a swath of flattened thistle between, tossing up detritus on either side like a haymow. From there it could have jagged north or zigzagged back in the direction from which it come. I wouldn't know where to begin.

Jeff blubbered as we worked. "I miss Mum and little Lily. Don't matter none if I hated the little snot when she was alive."

"Lily is alive," I snapped. "Big and little. I won't hear any more of that."

The boy regarded me sheepishly. "Judd Hancock says Mum

wasn't sucked into the air; he says she got divorced and went to California, her and little Lily. Is it true, Dad?"

"Tell you what, next time you see Judd Hancock break his nose for him."

"He'd prob'ly break mine."

The boy wiped his eyes on a sleeve and stared out at the sea, retreated deep into woods below the house, gleaming down there like a topaz mirror. He seemed to be relishing some hope.

"We're going to hear lots of crazy things. Don't you pay them any mind. We're men on our own here now. Men on their own can't afford to break down and cry."

"I never cried," he pouted, straddling one of the rafters left in place, kicking at air. "If another come, would it suck you in, Dad?" Adolescent's voice separating into two octaves. I was touched by its vulnerability, but didn't let on.

"According to Myrna Haney's theory, if a father and son twister come along it would likely take us both."

Jeff grinned. "That'd be pretty neat."

I looked away, recalling nightmares that sucked me in their woozy vortex each night on the threshold of sleep—dizzy, vertiginous spinwheels up into a black tunnel, 'round and 'round in a freight-train roar of diminishing spirals, until mouth swallowed feet and I disappeared into my own helixing guts. I would shout awake with Lily on my lungs. Drenched to the skin.

But you have to go on living

Still, I would not have done what I did next if I'd known how things would turn out. But you don't know, that's the point. You do what you think best—more often what you believe is better than worst. A boy shouldn't grow up without a woman's hand in the house, a man can't get by without her hand on his shoulder. There may be places don't believe it, but my household and Sluggard's Creek aren't among them. Twelve weeks after the Lilies disappeared, I set out to school with Jeffrey one morning to visit Lily Junior's teacher. I guessed I wouldn't be disrupting, since the school's windows weren't replaced yet and Jeff told me teachers spent the day rounding up papers and kids who slipped outside.

Standing at the head of the classroom beside a wall empty of windows, Miss Gilliam seemed like a porcelain doll when I peeked my head in the door. Every inch and feature of her delicate, miniaturized; fingernail rinds that skimmed her lips when she saw me no bigger than little Lily's. I stood fascinated as I'd been the first time I saw her, wondering as I had then if it was her smallness I lusted after in my heart or if I was just awestruck. "Come in," she chirped. "You're little, um—Mr. Connery—little, um, Lily's father," stifling a giggle. "Please— I'm sorry. I don't mean to be cruel." Blushing blue-pink, she turned to the blackboard, shoulders heaving. Every small head in the room looked back and forth in surprise.

Last fall at Meet the Teachers night, when she first heard Lily was named Junior, Miss Gilliam had laughed for minutes, catching her breath in whooping hiccups, perspiration seeping from a brow the wan blue of a gopher snake's belly. I thought I would have to administer the Heimlich maneuver. Then she threw back cinnamon-brown hair and composed herself. "M-most places, you know, m-most places people name sons Junior, not, um, daughters." I feared she would laugh again and that I would leap forward and kiss her tiny lips.

Big Lily glared at me, fathoming my thoughts. "This ain't most places," she snapped. *Why, she ain't nothing but a pale, sickly, not for nothing mosquito you wouldn't bother slapping,* her eyes said.

"No, no, I'm not against it. It's only, you see—people, um, up here—" Miss Gilliam hiccuped. Later, little Lily said her lips looked like wax candy.

"Teensy-weensy as they be, a tube of lipstick would last her a coon's age," big Lily had snarled.

Little Lily had explained in her gaspy way that Miss Gilliam didn't wear any lipstick. "She's all natural."

Now, Miss Gilliam turned agate-green eyes upon me, three matching creases in her brow. "Any word?" she inquired.

"No, ma'am. Nothing at all."

"We all miss Lily very much. Don't we children?"

"Yes, Miss Gilliam."

"We hope she will come back safe and sound."

"Yes, Miss Gilliam."

"Where could they be?" I demanded.

She stepped back against the desk. "Well I … really… I don't know. People do come back. The hostages, for example. What are the hostages' names, children?"

"Terry Anderson, Jesse Turner, Alann Steen," they intoned.

"Your wife and daughter, Mr. Connery—Lily, um, Junior and Senior—" laughter had fled upward into sinuses, leaving her forehead lucent "—they are hostages, too, in their way."

"How's that?"

"Hostages of the wind that won't reveal its secrets."

"Do you bake, Miss Gilliam?"

"What would I bake?"

"Pies, cinnamon rolls, that sort of thing. Men love cinnamon rolls."

"I'm afraid I don't follow."

"Not wishing to be rude, but I'd appreciate it if you could stop by some morning on your way to school and bake Jeffrey and me some cinnamon rolls. Or caramel. Whichever you prefer. I was hoping you might suggest it yourself."

"Oh. That's presumptuous of you."

I sensed the class coming alert, giggling and winking, making obscene signs to one another.

"Look, Miss, I'm not asking you to sleep in my wife's bed. Just the rolls. My boy misses them and I can't get it right."

"Children!" she snapped. "Jason Everbach, you better stop that. Where's Jillian?" A boy stood and wiggled his tongue at the girls' side. Miss G. was on him in a wink. A hammer blow atop the head and he deflated. Just as I'd expected: small as she was, she knew how to handle the male principle. She smiled, lips marzipan glossy. "Would you settle for Swedish pancakes with lingonberry butter?"

"I'd be more than grateful."

I took several spitballs on my way out, and knew by morning no one in town would pass the house without stopping to stare—as they had all along, only spiteful now instead of pitying. When it comes right down to it, what's the difference?

The honest truth is

I did not sleep with Miss Gilliam for six weeks. When I did it was Jeff suggested it. She had been coming around every morning to make breakfast. After I invited her to supper that first time—which I cooked myself—she came every evening. She would wash the dishes, then we would play hearts or watch television or she would help Jeffrey with his math homework; about ten she'd leave for home. I wondered what she had done with evenings in the past. She shrugged inside a peach blouse too big on her, fabric dimpling at shoulders. "Homework and things. Not much hot nightlife in Sluggard's Creek, I'm afraid."

We got arguing about how backward hill people are—so she claimed. I said if she heard the Haney sisters tell it, we are so wicked-worldly the Lord has taken to chastising us with tornados.

"You see what I mean—backwards!"

"You don't have to go to Teacher's College to look down on fussy old women," I said, mesmerized by her glazed cherry lips.

She snorted. "Would I be here if I looked down on people?" Glancing about—loose floor tiles, stairway boarded up, hutch lined with canned venison, pink and seemingly predigested chunks in brass-lidded Mason jars—she squirmed inside her clothes. Then started, seeing Jeff hidden in hallway shadows, eyes fixed on her in gleaming fascination ("She's so small," he kept saying). Miss Gilliam smiled at him.

"I tell my boy looking down on folks is risky business. We looked down on the gooks and they whipped us. Same with the Japs."

"Don't look down on me then."

"Me?"

"You should see yourself, really."

I felt my features.

"You know what your father told me, Jeffrey—" speaking to the door. "Men marry for cinnamon buns; women marry for common sense. I hope you aren't developing that attitude."

"Mom's were stickier between the cracks," said the doorway.

Miss Gilliam winced. "I'm sorry about your mother, Jeffrey. Really I am."

He emerged in his blue pajamas. "Is Miss Gilliam sleeping over tonight, Dad?"

"You better ask Miss Gilliam."

"Are you? It's dumb going clear home, then coming clear back every morning. The kids don't believe me anyway."

"Oh, they don't?"

He hung his head. "They say y'r an old maid."

"Oh, they do? One minute a slut, the next a spinster." She laughed as she had over Lily Junior, feathery hair soaking into her tea, beads of sweat popping like blood droplets across her velvety forehead. Swallowing sips of air, she fixed me with a steely uncompromising gaze. "We'll just show them. Those small snoopy-minded people you say I look down upon. We'll give 'em something to gossip about good." Her lips firmed, red as new-drawn blood.

"Not gossip," I stammered, "only rumors."

Thinking how long it had been since I had slept with another woman, I was scared limp. But Jeff's face tensed and resonated excitement; he undressed her shamelessly with his eyes. However, in the bathroom as we brushed our teeth he asked, "D'you think it's smart, Dad? She's so teensy. Mom was kinda big."

"I think you better mind your manners."

A tic caught the corner of his mouth as it did when he felt wronged. "She might break or somethin'," he muttered.

"They don't break easy. Besides, this was your idea."

He appeared confused, watching a blob of pink toothpaste spin down the drain. "I miss Mum and Lily a real lot."

"A man gets desperate," I reasoned. "That's how it hits him. Whether it's proper or improper, he doesn't know. Doesn't care. That's how he's made." Jeff wouldn't meet my eyes in the mirror.

"Don't take this wrong," Miss Gilliam said after we had made love and she lay draped more on the pillow than off of it. "I wouldn't have done this if I'd thought there was any chance, any chance at all…"

I touched a finger to her lips. "Me neither."

For the first time, I allowed myself to cry.

But didn't feel comfortable with the arrangement

We two took the Hide-A-Bed in the living room, making a cot for Jeffrey on the dining table. The bed sagged at one corner and squawked something awful when we made love, so Jeff next door was privy to everything. It must have embarrassed Miss Gilliam, discreet as she was. Each morning, she apologized to him for taking his side of the bed.

"You toss and turn a whole lot," he said.

She blushed. Always blue.

"Does she have real breasts, Dad?" he asked one morning before I left for work.

I tapped his nose. "Curiosity killed the cat."

"There's girls in my class bigger than her."

"Tits, you mean?"

He shrugged. "All over."

"Slow down, buster. You spend more of your life knowing about breasts and babies and cunnilingus than not knowing."

"What's cunnilingus?"

"What's the rush? Before he created man, God spent the first five and a half days working out sex. Pity to think he had nothing else on his mind before resting the seventh day."

"I'm only curious," Jeff said.

"Yeah, I suppose God was, too."

How it ended

What you learn is the whole story comes in a few moments. All the rest is preparation. This one came one Sunday morning in April. It was warm out; Miss Gilliam, whom I'd begun calling June, sat with me on the deck (she called it a deck: a few boards knocked together, hung off the rear of the house). She had gotten me interested in a mystery writer, Raymond Chandler, and we read his books, first June, then me. They got me wondering what became of the Lilies and what was the glue holding life together. Occasionally, we checked to see whether the sea—just a twinkle between treetops below—had disappeared completely as we expected it would any moment. "Then we'll be landlocked again," June would say.

Jeffrey came running around the house screeching at lungtop. "The Lilies are back, Mum and little. THEY COME HOME."

June and I exchanged a look. "Junior and senior," she whispered, her mouth a tiny, humorless hole.

"Holy stinking tomatoes."

"At least."

June closed her book and laid it on the chair, stood and walked across the deck, no taller standing than I was sitting down. It seemed downright improper I had slept with her; I couldn't understand why I had done it. Studying her narrow shoulders lost inside my old faded blue workshirt she liked to wear, tails reaching below her knees, I doubted I actually had. Of course

I hadn't. It would be like sleeping with a foster child I'd brought into my home who'd disguised herself as a woman. I recalled how last time I was at Melinda's restaurant she said the Lord had taken my Lilies away to test me. "I took you for a paltry sinner, Lawrence," she hissed, "I never expected filthiness." I wondered if big Lily had stopped by Melinda's before coming home.

June stood at the edge of the deck looking down at bracken fern thirty feet below. She turned and smiled fiercely, clapping her hands together. "Sooo, Jeffrey can have his cinnamon buns sticky between the cracks again." Her agate eyes glittered.

At that instant, Lily Junior appeared around the house, ponytails flopping. "Hi Daddy. Did you miss me?"

"Well, look who's here," I cried.

Seeing her chance, Junior kicked her brother in the shin and ran off screeching gleefully. You could see she had looked forward to this moment for weeks. Other than crook his knee to rub at the ankle, the boy ignored her, having outgrown all that. He gawked up at Miss Gilliam, whose shirt belled in the wind.

"You gonna jump?"

At that instant, Lily Senior's footsteps stalked through the house. I'd forgotten how heavily she walked. Once that tread comforted me; now it raised hairs on my neck. "Helloooo—" she called. Miss Gilliam's lips blanched vanilla, toes hung over the deck as if she would indeed jump, belly pressed to railing.

"Don't do it!" I cried. "I'll tell her about us, I promise—I'll— you'll see, I'll—" knowing there was nothing more to tell.

Below, Myrna Haney gloated up at me. "The Lord has returned your wife from the dead and found you in the arms of a harlot. He will have his comeuppance." She spat, eyeing Jeffrey as if he might cook up into a stew to satisfy a widow. He had positioned himself to catch Miss Gilliam if she jumped, his arms upstretched. Or maybe better to look up her shirt.

"Well, looky here!" Big Lily slammed the screen door behind

her, whumping a palm into the saddle of my back. "Just looky here." She was radiant, twenty pounds lighter, hair a leaning auburn corkscrew, eyeballs about to pop from sockets. They seemed to have found something—drink, or fear, or Jesus. "If it ain't the love of my life." Beaming, all of her distended—lips, eyes, arms—rubbery and bullfroggy. I rose to meet her embrace.

"I missed you, Lil...," words squeaking through the ache of my smile. Lily caught my shirt collar in one fist and floored me with a roundhouse blow of the other, popping a molar from its socket.

There was a squabble, barely discernible through a haze of semiconsciousness: the women going at it, Lily and June and Myrna Haney below. You wouldn't think a miniature schoolteacher could hold her own against a hundred and ninety irate, properly married pounds, but Miss Gilliam did. "You were dead!" she shouted. "You've got no business returning—"

"Do I look dead?"

"You're too fat to fit in heaven, too witless for hell."

"Red-lipped hussy!" Lily thundered, towering over her.

"Cow."

"Schoolteaching slut."

"Husband leaver."

"Why you ain't nothing but a weensy candy doll."

"Tornado wife." June leaned into her as if into a wind.

"You! Hah. No bigger than a shriveled rubber."

"Senior!"

Below, Myrna Haney did an impromptu samba, throwing arms in the air and shouting. A few neighbors joined her.

"Man snatcher—" Lily spied Jeffrey below "—CHILD MOLESTER."

"You think so, do you?" Forehead to forehead, back and forth

WILLIAM LUVAAS

across the planking, swallowing each other's words, Lily stomp-
ing and Miss Gilliam tiptoeing. A board gave way under Lily's
foot. She went through to the knee, down with a thump on her
buttocks. The deck shook, nails squealed out of walls on either
side; it lurched outward, yawning woozily on braces three feet
from the wall, tipped at an acute angle. My chair slid rapidly
down the deck, pinning my chest against the railing.

My women shot past me. Lily torpedoed headfirst under the
railing. June clipped it at the waist, cartwheeled over and spun
head over heels like a wheel, picking up speed down the incline
retreating water had left behind the house. Lily scooted on her
belly like a bobsled, cutting a trough down the red clay slope.
Both vanished into trees below, Jeffrey's shouts with them. He
paced the cliff edge, pounding fists against his hips.

Then, while I watched—pinned between chair back and
railing, feet kicking the air like a moth in a spider web—Myrna
Haney caught little Lily sack-fashion, feet and hands, and heaved
her over. Bumping, bouncing, shrieking until she was no more.
Myrna looked up at me. "A girl sooner be with her mother. You
wouldn't have no more use of her."

I gesticulated, sensing what was coming. But there might have
been a hairball lodged in my chest, I couldn't speak, ribs clamped
like fingers over my lungs. Jeffrey butted old Myrna in the
stomach. After an exhaled "ooof," she wore a look that was
nearly ecstatic. She caught my boy's hands, inviting him to dance
as she went over. Hands locked, they tumbled one over the other
down the mountain. "Whoooo—" Myrna cried, hanging in
midair above Jeff, who'd landed whump on his back against the
slope, "—eeeeee" as she flopped onto her back and wind rushed
out of her. "Whoooo—eeeeee. Whoooo—eeeeee."

A silence followed. Neighbors lined up along the precipice
and peered over. "Five souls lost in the space of a minute,"
Henry Staidly intoned solemnly. "That's worse than the storm
itself."

Far below, the sea had ceased to twinkle.

And how I did
They had to call in a ladder truck from Haneyville and disassemble the deck to get me down. I kicked and bit their hands, hoping volunteers would drop me over the slope to join my family. They grinned and cried "hot damn," like I was a bee's nest they were determined to remove from the tree despite the stings. The fire chief stood with his lieutenant at the edge of the slope discussing plans for retrieving the bodies below.

Someone permitted Melinda to ride along in the back of the ambulance with me. Flushed and stalwart. Later I would learn that at first news of her sister's death she had collapsed to her knees and sung praise of the Lord in a velvety baritone, with an enthusiasm that caused her half-converted kitchen help to quit on the spot. Melinda's dry palms caressed my cheeks, she smelled of flour and cinnamon, her eyes gleamed moisture, while the thumping of her heart caused her huge bosom to expand and fold, expand and fold. I couldn't budge my eyes from it.

"Now, our Lawrence," she said, "maybe you are ready to get serious. You have outlived the Lilies twice over. You wouldn't dare tempt the Lord a third time."

I found I could not speak with ribs caging my lungs. I nodded and bit clean through my lip. Blood wet my chin and soaked into the starch-stiff sheet in which I was cocooned, osmosing downward. With any luck it would reach my toes. I looked into Melinda's greasy bloodshot eyes and nodded, believing it better to salvage something than to navigate this sad planet with nothing at all.

Jiri Kajanë

*My brother Serxhe is on the left; I'm on the right. Our
friend Ana, the pretty one, came between us.*

Jiri Kajanë (b. 1947) was raised in Krujë, Albania, and trained in engineering
at Tiranë University in the late 1960s. He is the author of a number of stories,
including the collection *Sa Kushtón (What Is the Cost?)*, and over a dozen one-
act plays. His satirical drama *Nesër Përditë (Tomorrow, Everyday)* received great
acclaim in a singular 1981 performance before being banned. Due to Kajanë's
precarious standing before the revolution and the country's industrial paralysis
that followed, "Leni Calls Me for Advice" has never been formally published
in Albania. This is his first English translation.

JIRI KAJANË
Leni Calls Me for Advice
Translated from Albanian
by Kevin Phelan and Bill U'Ren

*L*eni calls me for advice. All the time. It could be
three in the morning, maybe on a Tuesday, a workday, and the
phone will ring. "Hello," I'll say.

"It's me," Leni will announce, and then he'll go straight into
it, whatever it is. Never any small talk, no introductions, not
even a word to bring us back to where we left off or quickly
remind me of our most recent discussion.

This past Tuesday, Leni was calling about a rabbit, a very soiled
and lifeless rabbit. At first, it surprised me, although I am not sure
why. Maybe I expected him to jump into a conversation about
Lena, an older lady he's begun seeing, or maybe it was just
because he telephoned me at the office. I receive very few calls
at work these days, so even the sound of the telephone ringing
can catch me off guard. In fact, despite my many years of
experience as the minister of slogans, lately I have found myself
with rather little to do here. And, as I have recently discovered,
this can become quite a vicious cycle—when you are out of
favor, you are rarely granted programs, and when you do not
have programs, you always receive a bad evaluation. This has
happened to me, and even fairly quickly I might add.

As usual, Leni was in a bit of a panic when he called. While the rabbit he spoke of had definitely been dead for hours and possibly days, he seemed convinced that there wasn't a moment to lose. Time was crucial. And strangely enough, he thought contacting me would somehow bring the animal back to life— that maybe I could list for him a series of actions that would resurrect the creature. And maybe he imagined I'd illustrate these options with some entertaining and carefully worded slogans, since I certainly had the time on my hands to devote to such a project.

Of course I didn't actually possess this scientific—or perhaps even spiritual—knowledge, but Leni was not prepared to accept "I don't know" as my final answer. Since I had never given him that response before, I could understand his reluctance. On the other hand, his previous inquiries for advice had revolved solely around matters of the heart, not those of life and death, so it wasn't as if I had a prototype to follow.

For a moment, I thought about explaining that with his usual questions, the ones concerning women, there truly were no right or wrong answers. Okay, maybe there were some wrong answers, but realistically there were a lot more in-between, gray areas, things that could go either way. Percentagewise, it was almost always a lopsided battle where, at best, you could only cut your losses. With the present query, however, there was none of that vagueness—it was simply a right and wrong situation. Unfortunately, my area of expertise, I like to think, lies in questions that require longer, more subjective answers, answers with plenty of room for discourse and rationalization, so, as you can see, I was quite at a loss for words.

"What should I do? What should I do? What should I do?" Leni kept saying. It was evident that I had no choice but to resort to the decision-making skills that I had perfected years ago when I'd first been recruited—the main tactic of which seemed to revolve around stalling.

"Okay, tell me everything from the start," I said.

54

"Mr. Kruchnik left Friday morning," Leni began, "and I was supposed to be at his place that night, but I couldn't. Kiti had telephoned from Pogradec and said she really needed me to come down."

Let me outline the situation in a little more detail. Leni works as the driver for a rising leader in the party, a job he was appointed to recently, and one that many would consider a big break. His boss, Mr. Kruchnik, is a young man, much younger than I, almost the same age as Leni, but he is very powerful. Often, he is required to travel outside of the country and when this happens he hires a man to look after his home, pets, and garden. This most recent trip, however, arose on very short notice. So, while en route to the train station, he asked Leni to accept the responsibility of temporary caretaker. Leni said okay—what else could he say?—and that is where things stand at the moment.

As far as Kiti goes, she and Leni had been romantically involved a while back until, unfortunately, a problem surfaced. With a small loan of hard currency, I was able to effect a resolution to that situation, and Leni was able to move on. For further details, I would have to consult my notes.

Leni continued: "Kiti phoned that morning from Pogradec and said she needed me to come down. As you know, I cannot refuse her. Kiti has that way, that voice—you understand."

I did understand. Almost a year before, I had the opportunity to make Kiti's acquaintance on a ferry to Sarande. I had to agree, she was a very strong woman.

"When I returned home the next day, I was met at my door by Nossi." This is Leni's older brother. A somewhat capable man, Nossi has recently gotten in a little over his head at the dairy. "He begged for my help on his route," Leni added. "What could I do?"

It was quickly becoming apparent that he wasn't going to slow down, so I started to take notes.

"Nossi introduced me to Ivo, and Ivo introduced me to

Lilliana—whom I must tell you about soon, but not now. Anyway, by that time it was far too late for traveling the great distance to Mr. Kruchnik's home, especially along that unlit road through Vlorë—you know how it is. So I waited until the next morning. Unfortunately, I had not realized that the car was low on fuel, and the tanks at the service station were empty. I waited for a long time, almost three hours, but the filling truck did not come. I called many people before discovering that my friend Avdo had a supply of twenty liters, but he wasn't interested in parting with the fuel. We talked for many hours, and I reminded him of all the times I had helped him. I especially reminded him of the tools you had lent me to lend him for the construction of his cousin's dacha. Finally, he agreed, and I was able to make the journey."

My notes quickly required diagrams and flow charts. I broke out the coveted set of ink pens I'd obtained from an art student in trouble last summer.

"When I arrived at Mr. Kruchnik's, things weren't as I had been told. Sure there was a house, still safe, and a pool, now filled with leaves, and yes, even a dog, a quite hungry dog, in fact. But there was something more. In the yard, next to the dog's quarters amidst the torn-up lawn, there was a beige rabbit that was now brown, due to the dirt, and red, due to the blood." Leni paused. "The rabbit was dead. His cage door was open, his food bowls were gone, and his water bottle had disappeared, too." There was another pause.

"So?" I prodded.

"Maybe the dog got hungry," he said. "When I didn't show up with his kibble, perhaps he opened the rabbit's cage and killed it. For food, I think." There was a pause. "Mr. Kruchnik never mentioned anything about a rabbit, you know."

I stopped taking notes, realizing that my part in this situation was about to arrive.

"It is not an entirely unjustified reaction from a dog's point of view," Leni added, in the absence of anything from my end. "The dog was just following his natural instincts."

"So, Leni," I cut in, still trying to devise an even remotely acceptable plan, "precisely what shape is the rabbit in?"

"He seems to be more than a little dead," Leni responded in all seriousness.

"No, I mean, how badly has he been eaten?"

"Not badly at all. It looks like he just got dragged through the dirt for a while. At least I was here in time to stop that."

"Good," I said. In the past, this was usually where I offered Leni my answer. By the time he'd finish explaining a problem, I'd almost always have a plausible solution prepared. Then I would offer it in plain terms, and he would accept. "Thank you," he would usually say.

Tonight, however, I was not quite so sure. My brain seemed to be moving pretty slowly, almost in stop time, and I felt myself concentrating just a little too hard. I couldn't compile any actual options for him, let alone begin the process of deducing, so I was mostly left with the choice of improvising—thinking out loud. Still, Leni wouldn't recognize that I was stalling, and so his confidence in me would be preserved.

"You have three choices," I said, although I no idea if this were really true. On the average, there are usually three solutions to every problem, so it seemed reasonable enough. I'd just have to invent them as I went along.

"One," I started, using my hands even though Leni couldn't see them, "is that you explain the entire situation to Mr. Kruchnik when he returns, and beg for mercy." There was a silence, and I could tell that Leni was anxious for the second option. Honesty had never served him well in the past, and so there was really no precedent to push him in that direction.

"Two, you could replace the rabbit with one that looks just like it, and hope that Mr. Kruchnik won't be able to tell the difference. With his hectic schedule, it is hard to imagine he has much time for pets anyway.

"Or three, you could wash the rabbit off, put it back in the cage, and pretend that nothing has happened."

There was an uncharacteristically long silence after that. I was not sure whether Leni was mulling over the possibilities or just waiting to hear which choice I would personally recommend. After nearly a minute passed, I ventured a solution. "Number three," I said, simply. I had no idea whether this was the best answer, but I did know that it was the one Leni wanted to hear. In the past, we had had a lot of success using the "ignore it and hope it goes away" approach. Besides, the first solution wasn't a genuine possibility, and the second would cost hard currency that I did not have and could not, therefore, lend. "Number three is the best."

"Okay. You're sure?"

"Yes, Leni," I offered weakly, not too certain about any part of this unique situation. "Besides, there is no way they can prove anything that happened was your fault. They aren't going to have a doctor examine the rabbit, right?"

"I suppose not."

"All you have to do is give it a good washing, tidy up the yard, drop in a water bottle and maybe some food, then slide him into the cage," I said, adopting an almost instructional tone. "And simply claim everything was fine when you left," I cautioned, rehearsing him. "That's all you have to say."

"Right," Leni answered, quietly trying to build his confidence.

"They'll have to assume you've done a perfect job, performing every duty to its fullest—feeding the dog and rabbit, watering the lawn, bringing in the mail and packages, everything. Then, possibly sometime between your departure and their arrival, the rabbit must have died—a heart attack, right in his cage. It is that simple.

"And Leni," I added, before we got off the line. "Make sure

you leave out a large bowl of dog food this time."

A day or two passed, and I had even less work at the office than before. Killing time, I tried thinking up a few slogans for myself, hoping to keep my skills sharp and maybe just brighten my outlook. Unfortunately, I had trouble coming up with anything good. A few of the classics, all from the West, kept popping into my mind, clogging the path for anything new. "The clash of ideas is the sound of freedom." "There can be no happiness if the things we believe in are different from the things we do." "Correction does much, but encouragement does more." "I hate my job and I'm afraid I will lose it." After about an hour, I gave up and decided to head out for an early lunch, since no one was going to miss me anyway.

I took a patio table at the nearby Hotel Durrës and ordered a cup of oriz më tamel, the house rice pudding, and some coffee. It was early, maybe eleven o'clock or so, and the breakfast I had eaten that morning certainly had been enough, but I still needed to get out of the office.

After the waiter dropped off some cream and sugar, I began rereading the paper to see if I'd missed anything earlier. The front page was covered with the usual "feel-good" stories— from a woman saving her baby during a boating mishap, to the pride one farmer's boy felt for his bicycle. All were calculated to keep everyone's mind off the real news, or the possibility of real news. The press was still ignoring actual events, especially international ones, in the same way that they had been ordered to do in the past. Often, such censorship (through oversight) was the subject of debate among the city's intellectuals at night in the square. I used to laugh when I heard them in the coffeehouses, wildly conjecturing and pontificating. Inside, I was content to know the truth of the matter, what was really going on. Sometimes I used to feel superior with this knowledge of clandestine events, even the most trivial. But that time has passed.

JIRI KAJANË

Before my recent descent into disfavor at work, I'd been privy
to nearly each and every inside story at the office, whether it was
truth or rumor. One time, I had even been invited by the
original minister of communication to watch American television at the Palace of Culture in Skënderbeg Square. I believe one
show we saw was about a psychiatrist and his unusual patients,
and I spent the entire evening seated in the front row, laughing
along with the heads of state. Of course, that was a few years
back, when my value as an employee of the party was at its peak.
Now, I can take a two- or three-hour lunch and no one misses
me.

In the newspaper's "world ideas" section, there was a column
written by a British golfer who had quit the pro tour due to its
"distorted morals and the claustrophobic upper-class lifestyle."
Originally, it continued, he came from a working-class background, learning golf on the public courses. As expected, the
article highlighted each and every aspect of the player's decision
to leave the capitalist pro tour. The part I found most interesting,
however, was his approach to the game itself. His best days on
the green had usually been the days when he went just by
instinct—not thinking about his upcoming round and not
taking practice swings. "Sometimes if I am completely preoc-
cupied, I'll usually birdie a good portion of holes, and par the
rest. But when I have nothing on my mind except the game, I'll
overanalyze everything—the course, sand traps, my swing, even
to the point of worrying about what shoes I was wearing—and
end up playing like hell."

At around noon, I signed my tab and headed toward down-
town, thinking that a walk through the old marketplace might
help me forget about work and perhaps overcome the block
unconsciously. It wasn't until I reached Maligni Ruga that it
occurred to me how unseasonably cold it was. At first, I thought
it might rain, but again, I was just being fooled by the combi-
nation of the gray sky and faded concrete buildings playing on

my senses. Most of the time, the day would end the same as it started, no rain and no sun, just somewhere in between.

Near the inverted fountain, dry now for the last decade, surveyors had marked the site of Hoxha's newest statue with white chalk and wooden stakes. As I walked over to rest on one of the marble benches, I was cut off in the street by Leni. He had been running madly, sweating through his suit, and didn't seem to recognize me. As I brushed him off with my handkerchief, his eyes refocused.

"Mr. Kruchnik has released me," he said, wiping some dirt off his mouth. "I have been expelled from the party." Leni's caretaking incident involving the rabbit quickly came back to me, and I realized that our plan had obviously failed.

"Why? He can't do that, can he?" I asked in a calm tone, trying to reassure him.

"Apparently so," Leni said, distracted. "But now if you'll excuse me."

"Where are you going, Leni?"

"To beg for Kruchnik's mercy, to beg for my old job back."

"Let me go with you," I said, fixing my collar. "I will straighten this out."

When we got to Kruchnik's building, across the river and near the old mosque, Leni seemed to regain a bit of his composure. We washed up in the lobby bathroom, then proceeded to traverse the maze of corridors to Kruchnik's wing.

"Hello," he answered, barely opening the door. "What can I do for you?" He was holding a small bottle of mineral water and wearing some type of coat, or odd smoking jacket, along with his spectacles. I assumed he'd been reading the paper.

"Mr. Kruchnik," Leni started, "I am here to apologize for what has happened. I am terribly sorry. You must understand."

"Apology accepted," Kruchnik said, cutting Leni off. "But it is *you* who must understand that I cannot reinstate you as my driver. And as for the party itself, well ... I have left that matter up to Mr. Xherxhe down the hall."

"But Mr. Kruchnik," I interjected, with a tone of dignity to remind him of my own place in the party. "Isn't this a bit drastic? After all, wouldn't it be reasonable to assume such a thing could have happened with or without Leni's presence?"

"I see your reasoning, sir," he said, putting his bottle of water down on a small wooden stand next to the door. "But I don't think you have the entire story straight. In fact, I am sure you don't, otherwise you would not have come along like this to embarrass yourself." I didn't react, trying hard to keep my expression vague so as not to reveal my confusion. Kruchnik continued, "When my family and I returned from our trip, and my daughter found her rabbit in his old cage like that, I cannot begin to tell you— If you could have seen the look on her face..." he said, trailing off. "After all, this is the second time we've had to bury him, and I consider that to be one time too many. Now good day to both of you."

The door slammed in our faces, and the two of us stood there in the empty hallway, Leni and I, bewildered by this ridiculous truth that had just been revealed. I thought about how odd it must have looked to Mr. Kruchnik, how strange it might have seemed that Leni would dig up the family rabbit from its simple grave in the backyard, shampoo it in the bath, and dry its hair

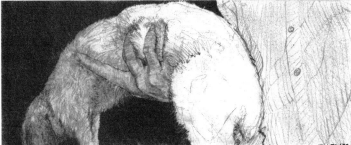

until it had regained that original fluffy glow. I thought about how chilling it must have been for his daughter to find her dead pet back in its old cage with some food and water. The absurdity of it, both the situation and our luck, could only make me laugh. We had tried to cover a mistake that had never even been made.

Then, for the first time in weeks, I was able to see the solution to a problem almost instantaneously. I knocked on Kruchnik's door, hoping for a chance to try it on him right away, and then dispatched Leni down to the waiting area, assuring him that it would be better if I handled this alone. A moment later, Kruchnik answered. He seemed angry this time, at least outwardly angry, so I tried to explain as quickly as possible, before he could slam the door again.

It had been my fault, I began. Leni's brother was injured in an accident that weekend, and I had offered to perform Leni's duties while he stayed with Nossi in the hospital. Unfortunately, I had been careless in fulfilling them, and, therefore, Leni was not to blame.

Mr. Kruchnik seemed puzzled by my sudden confession. Not so much by the fact that I'd been involved in the first place, that didn't seem to shock him, but more by the fact that I would sacrifice myself so willingly. Kruchnik seemed perplexed, perhaps concluding that, of the two of us, I had much more to lose than Leni, who was still young and inexperienced. And yet here I was, practically throwing it all away. Clearly, I had gotten his attention.

"I'm curious," Kruchnik began, absentmindedly touching his temple with the palm of his hand. "I'm curious about your role in this. Explain it to me in detail, if you will."

I assured Kruchnik that nothing would make me happier and began spinning the story's particulars off the top of my head. As I spoke, I felt a sudden freedom—like being released from gravity, no longer having to protect what little social standing I had left. The story seemed only to build as it progressed quickly from my mind, with each detailed component stacking neatly upon the previous one. Almost effortlessly, I weaved some of

Leni's original facts into a more believable, and even more entertaining, story—despite the fact that it was being invented at that very moment. I could see clearly that Mr. Kruchnik was enthralled and, to be honest, I was not surprised. But as I finally brought it all to a tidy conclusion, he didn't appear to betray any reaction. He just stood there, staring out toward the marble balcony, with its great view of the mosque in the distance.

"So," Kruchnik finally began, appearing to ease up a little, "let me understand. You mean to tell me that you went to all the trouble of actually washing this dead rabbit, shampooing it even, just to conceal your negligence?"

I stood there in silence, not really sure if it was actually a question or, for that matter, what response it would merit if it were. Instead, I thought about the small room in which I've lived all these years, how sparse it is, and how little time I've actually spent there. I thought about the hat-check girl at the Hotel Durrës, the beautiful young one whom Leni managed to see from time to time, and whom I myself had once invited to a party function, only without much luck. And I thought about the day I'd been stuck on that train up north, delayed for thirty-eight hours, waiting for the winter storm to pass over Shkoder. I remembered how difficult it was to sleep in the cramped compartment I shared with those three young students—about how I was left sitting there staring at them as they rested effortlessly through the night.

"I want both of you to come by this evening for a drink," Kruchnik stated plainly. "Please be at my house around seven."

"Very good, sir," I answered, and before turning to leave, he put out his hand.

"Have you ever considered working for the minister of information?" he asked, stepping back from the door. "I know it would seem like a demotion in some people's eyes, but in the long run..." he trailed off. "Perhaps we could discuss it tonight."

On the way back, Leni talked about how he would have to call his brother Nossi to make sure they got the new story straight, matching the details word for word with what I had told Kruchnik. He even discussed the possibility of intentionally denting Nossi's truck, just to be on the safe side. I weighed his idea for a moment, then told him it would not be necessary. I was certain that if the situation did arise, I would be able to think of something far less damaging.

From there, Leni agreed to accompany me back to my department before we headed over to Nossi's for a little celebration. Upstairs, the entire floor of the office was deserted and the only sign of life was a flashing red light on the telex machine. I guided Leni down the long hallway and into the corner office that has been mine for these past twelve years. At first, I think he was a little surprised at how barren it all was, or maybe it was just the way the large room and high ceilings seemed to dwarf my small, aging desk. "Oh," he said. "Nice."

Quickly, I rustled through the papers in my box, hoping to find something new—perhaps a note from one of my colleagues, a memorandum from a party official, or even just a message from my secretary. But there was nothing, only the precise pile of papers that I'd seen earlier that morning and, quite possibly, the morning before that. "We can go now," I mumbled in Leni's direction. Soon, though, I thought to myself, I will have to break this bad habit of checking in with an office that clearly does not miss me.

Outside, we headed north toward Nossi's, past the shell of the old train station, and up into the surrounding hills, decorated now only by failed crops and deserted concrete bunkers. It went on that way for five or six miles. Empty and gray. And, as always, I looked forward to the working street lamp at the edge of Krujë, the one that signals the beginning of town. It stands there alone, continuously lit, the simple yellow bulb glaring brightly through the cracked glass sphere that surrounds it.

Melanie Bishop

*Life at its best, then and now: A favorite pillow, fuzzy pajamas,
beverage of choice, and someone to make me smile.*

Melanie Bishop has an M.F.A. in fiction from the University of Arizona. She's
been the recipient of a *Transatlantic Review* Award, a Chesterfield Screenwriting
Fellowship, and a Tennessee Williams Scholarship to last summer's Sewanee
Writers' Conference. Her work has appeared in *Florida Review, Puerto del Sol,
Greensboro Review,* and *Love's Shadow,* an anthology of writing by women.

Bishop lives in Prescott, Arizona, and teaches writing and literature at Prescott
College.

MELANIE BISHOP
Sisterhood

*J*zzy and I are sitting outside of TimeSaver, drinking
our daily Icees. If you collect stickers off the cups littered around
the parking lot, you can turn them in and get your Icee for free.
Fifteen stickers gets you a small, any flavor.

My brother Jake, who taught me about the stickers, no longer
collects them himself. I didn't know this till the other day when
Mom took us all school shopping at the mall and bought us Icees
when we were done. Jake finished his and tossed the cup in one
of those garbage cans with the swinging trapdoor.

"Jake," I said, "the sticker!"

He shrugged.

"I'll get it," I said. He's the one who'd taught me how you
could lift the whole head off those mall garbage cans, their
swinging doors like big mouths. I went for the cup.

"Johanna!" he said. His voice was quiet but sharp, and the way
he shook his head like my dad does let me know I was doing
something very wrong. A year before, I swear he would've done
the same thing—I'd seen him dig through Dumpsters.

But now girls call him at home, even though he is almost never
there and you have to take messages. "Call Rita." "Call Grace."
"Would you please tell him to call Monique? It's very important."
I never see him with these girls, don't even have faces in my head

to match the names, because these people go to the high school, and I just wrapped up junior high.

TimeSaver has a history for me and Izzy. We were here for the grand opening years ago, when she was in second grade and I was in third. That day they closed off the street, had a Dixieland band in the parking lot, and some players from the New Orleans Saints signing autographs. Izzy and I came every day of every summer vacation since, and cola Icees are to me what milk is supposed to be to kids. They're making my bones strong.

At night, the TimeSaver parking lot is transformed. Older kids from the high school pull in and out for cigarettes and Boone's Farm, couples mostly and double dates. Cars collect, people talk to each other with their windows down till the cops come and clear everyone out. Eventually, they just assemble again. I know this not from the experience of having been in one of these cars. I have never been on a date, to the TimeSaver parking lot or anywhere. But when Izzy spends the night at my house, where there is less supervision than at hers, we sneak out late and ride our bikes down here for midnight Icees. If you're on a bike, forget about being part of that crowd. You have to be in a car.

In the cars, they pour rum in their cola Icees. Rum and Coke is a well-known drink. We've also seen people pour something into the cherry Icees—clear, so we figure it's vodka, but neither of us knows the name of this drink. We know about vodka from the screwdrivers Izzy's parents drink on Saturday mornings. Orange juice. Or put the vodka in tomato juice and call it a Bloody Mary. We watch carefully when we're at TimeSaver. As long as you're there, it's important to learn something. There's a lot we don't know.

I have a new crush on a guy that works behind the counter. His name is Scott, which I know only because he wears a name tag. It's getting to the point where if we walk or ride down here and he's not working, it feels like a wasted trip. Today is one of those days. Used to be, I was satisfied with the Icees, and an occasional Reese's cup.

"You done?" Izzy says. She's usually ready to leave before I am. But with Scott not around, what's the point of staying?

"I guess." I tear the diamond-shaped proof-of-purchase stickers off my cup and drop them in the candy bag, with the ones she's already torn off of hers. We jump down from the concrete wall we always sit on, just as a car screeches through the parking lot and comes to a bucking stop next to us. Four boys are inside.

"What have we here?" one of them says. And then the driver honks, so close we can't help but jump.

"Keep walking," I whisper to Izzy. We pretend they aren't there.

The car moves slowly next to us, at the same pace we walk. Their radio is loud, and one guy in the back is singing. We head into the pharmacy, even though we don't need anything there.

The boys start barking and the car peels out, while someone yells "Dogs!" and someone else howls like a coyote.

"Idiots," Izzy says. Quietly, to me.

When we turn onto our street, I see a car I don't recognize in front of my house, and then three girls, all dressed up, walking away from our front porch. They start to get in the car, just as we walk up.

"Johanna?" the driver says.

I say yes, but I have never seen any of these girls in my life. One of them hands me an envelope. I'm wearing the cutoffs that I accidentally cut uneven, with the rainbow patch on the butt. I'm barefoot, and my big toe has a Band-Aid on it where I constantly stub it.

"It's an invitation," the blonde girl says. "Have you heard of Theta Row?"

I shake my head. My teeth feel sticky from the Sugar Daddy I just finished eating.

The same girl keeps doing the talking, tells me that I'm being rushed for a high school sorority, and all the rushes are invited to a pool party at her house.

I open the invitation and see the words Theta Rho, not spelled r-o-w the way I imagined. I stare at this and can come up with nothing to say. I nod.

"I'm Alice, the vice-president," the girl continues. "And this is Cindy and Monique. They're both senior members and they're coordinating rush this year."

Just then Jake walks out of the house and their attention is diverted, and for the first time I'm able to look at Izzy. She looks as confused as I feel.

"Jake," the one named Monique says. She walks toward him, and everything about her clothes is perfect. Then I realize I have seen her working at the Holmes store at the mall. The outfit is right off a mannequin.

Jake pushes his hair back and smiles. Doesn't matter if he doesn't say anything because he is cute and he knows it. They all say hi and Izzy and I step back a little.

Jake takes the invitation from my hand and points to the symbols on the front, like a strange monogram. "Those are Greek letters," he says to me.

"I know," I lie.

The girls lean against the car, and Jake with them, and me and Izzy know it's our cue to get lost.

"Well, thanks," I say.

"Yeah," the vice-president says. "We'll see you next Sunday."

That night I get all the details from my older sister, Laura, who still lives at home, even though she's one year out of high school. She says she wasn't Theta Rho material, but anyone who's been to that high school knows all about it. It's the girls who go out with the football players, the girls who get stuff like homecoming queen.

"You're not Theta Rho material, either," she says. "Trust

me."

My mother tells her to be nice.

"I'm just being honest," she says. "These girls have cars and gorgeous clothes. They're cheerleaders. They're popular."

"So?" my mother says.

"So … Johanna? Come on."

"Laura," my mom says.

"I'm not trying to be mean. But, it's probably some mistake. She's not their type."

"Neither were you, then," I say, knowing I have my mother on my side.

"I didn't want to be. There's a difference."

Izzy stays over that night, and after everyone's in bed we get out of our nightgowns and put our jeans back on. I wear my favorite poor-boy shirt, that accentuates what little I have. Izzy French-braids my hair, and we sneak out the sliding glass door, much quieter than sneaking out the front. Our bikes are waiting. We used to call them our horses, but we've outgrown this. We walk them silently to the street, get on, and ride away without making a sound. At the corner, a safe distance, we let out our usual holler.

These are our best moments. It's not cool outside, but just the absence of the daytime heat is a sort of freedom. And the mosquitoes, less at night anyway, can't catch you when you're on your bike, not as fast as we go. MacArthur Boulevard, full of traffic during the day, is still this late at night, and wet from a brief shower. The air is thick like honey and there is only the sound of our tires on wet pavement. When we make the final turn onto Kabel Drive, long and straight and newly blacktopped, we ride without hands, a tradition. Side by side. No fear. The road is smooth as cream-cheese frosting.

We put our hands on the handlebars only at the last minute, to maneuver the turn into TimeSaver.

Immediately, I see that the white-shirted boy behind the night-shift counter is Scott. We've brought along thirty stickers, worth two Icees, but when we see him we put those away and take enough quarters out of our pockets to cover it. I send Izzy in and I wait on the concrete wall.

"What'd he say?" I ask her when she comes out.

"Nothing," Izzy says. "He just took the money."

I start explaining everything Laura said to me. About how rush is the step before pledge, the time where they decide if they like you enough to make you a pledge. I tell her how pledge is supposed to be hell, and lasts three months, but then you're in. Izzy nods.

"Do you know any of these girls?" she asks.

"Not yet," I tell her. "But I'm thinking if I make it, then next year I could get you in."

"I don't know," Izzy says.

I can't blame Izzy for feeling this way. She's gone to Catholic schools all her life, and won't go to public until she's in tenth grade. She can't know what it's like in public. You need all the help you can get. Theta Rho is like a ticket to almost everything, the difference between a great time and a miserable time, for three whole years of your life.

"Well, we'll see," I say. "I'll check it out for you."

The older kids start to race through the parking lot. It is a cool thing to slam on your brakes, and to talk to people in another car while both cars are still running. To occasionally step on the gas, even though the car is parked. Every car that pulls in has on the same radio station, WTIX. It's the one we listen to, too. I know the disc jockeys by name, and have spoken to them on the request line.

It's different this late at night. The kids in the cars don't bother us and we don't bother them. You get points just for being out, no matter how old you are. And people act different when they're on a date, like they're playing grown-up or something.

Any of these guys might holler something at us during the day, but not while their arms are wrapped around their girlfriends.

After they've all bought their Icees and are secretly concocting drinks in their cars, I get up the nerve to walk in the store and get a look at Scott. Izzy comes with me. We're quiet as we walk up and down the aisles. We check out the new *Seventeen*, read our horoscopes and the advice column. I sneak a glance at myself in the shoplifter mirrors, angled in each corner of the store. I try to think if I did have the guts to say something to Scott, what would it be? What would Alice say, or Cindy, or Monique? I look toward the cash register, and he's not even looking at us; he's sweeping behind the counter.

We go to the candy counter where we find a new kind of gum that must've just come in. Called hot-dog gum, it's red, individually wrapped, and shaped like you would imagine. Izzy picks one up and we look at each other, having the same thought. I dare her to buy one. She says no way. I hold one at an angle, down at my crotch, and we both burst out laughing and have to run out of the store.

"Oh, my God," we say. We catch our breath. We watch more cars come and go.

At one o'clock TimeSaver closes, and we decide to wait till then. It's only twenty more minutes, and the plan is I will say good night to Scott as he locks up and leaves.

Izzy listens while I practice. "Try more cheerful," she says, and I do. "Good, now a little more confident," she says.

I practice these two words till they don't sound like real words anymore. Good night. Good night.

He comes out before we expect him, to sweep up the cigarette butts out front. A girl from one of the cars calls to him: "Scott!" He walks over to the car, leans on the broom while he talks to them. Somebody lights one cigarette off another one and hands it to him. He smokes. We keep sipping our Icees, which have mostly melted, because of how long we're having to make them last.

"He has a cute butt," I whisper.

"Yeah," Izzy says.

When he finishes talking to the people in the car, he heads back toward where we sit, but doesn't look at us. He takes a last puff of his cigarette, so close to us we can smell it, then he drops it on the ground and smushes it with his shoe. When he does this, there is a moment where he and I look right at each other. I try to smile. It's too early to say good night and I haven't prepared anything else. Izzy elbows me to say something.

"Hi," I say.

He looks us over.

"Isn't it past y'all's bedtime?" he says.

We get up to go and he keeps sweeping.

As we ride home, we don't talk or laugh. We make our turns out of habit. We keep our hands on the handlebars.

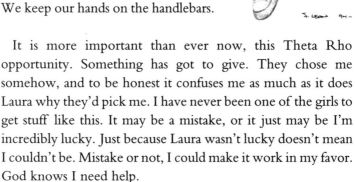

It is more important than ever now, this Theta Rho opportunity. Something has got to give. They chose me somehow, and to be honest it confuses me as much as it does Laura why they'd pick me. I have never been one of the girls to get stuff like this. It may be a mistake, or it just may be I'm incredibly lucky. Just because Laura wasn't lucky doesn't mean I couldn't be. Mistake or not, I could make it work in my favor. God knows I need help.

My mother says it's not important to be popular. Whenever I'm getting ready for a school dance, or a party I'm nervous about, she always says the same thing: "Just be yourself and they'll love you." This is not as easy as it sounds, nor is it necessarily true. One, no one has made it clear to me exactly who "myself" is, and two, even when you think for a minute that you know, like I did when I said hi to Scott, somebody can set you straight.

Izzy has some deal after church that Sunday, so I'm stuck getting ready for the swim party without her help. Laura comes into the room we share, while I'm getting dressed.

"I hope that's not what you're wearing," she says.

"Maybe," I say. It was what I planned to wear till she said that.

"Jo," she says, "you've had that for about three years."

"It still fits," I say. It's a beach dress, to be worn over a bathing suit. It has sailboats and starfish on it and the handle to the zipper is a blue metal anchor.

"It doesn't do anything for you."

Laura flips through my clothes in the closet, then her own. She has never once let me wear something of hers.

"Try this," she says, like she's already exasperated. She throws the outfit on my bed. It is one she made last year, shorts with a matching shirt. "You won't exactly fill it out," she says, "but it'll be an improvement over that sailor dress. Jesus, throw that thing away."

It was only two years ago that I was not allowed to cross a line down the center of our room, a line that Laura had marked with masking tape. And she has always been possessive with her things. I'm not comfortable with her new generosity.

"You sure?" I say.

"Just be careful with it. Don't spill on it or anything."

I stand on the toilet in the bathroom, which is the only place you can get a full-length view. I turn sideways. The outfit looks decent, anyway, if my legs weren't so skinny. And the bikini top under the shirt helps create the illusion of something there. Jake and his friends have names for girls' stages of development. First is the raisin stage, then pancakes, then fried eggs, then peaches, grapefruits, and melons. They used to say this to us when we'd walk by. "You getting a leap on the raisin stage there, Jo?" Nobody ever teases guys about their things, which I imagine to be pale and puny and damp.

I'm seeing if the shirt looks better tucked in or out, when Jake knocks hard on the door, twice.

"Unlock the door, Jo," he says. "I gotta get something."

I open the door and he takes his comb out of the drawer and sticks it in his back pocket.

"Your Theta Rho thing is today?" he says.

"Uh-huh."

"You look good."

"What?"

"You're starting to look better in your clothes," he says.

"This is Laura's," I say.

I hoped for a ride to this affair, but my mother is suddenly gone with the car, my father is watching football, and I don't dare ask Laura for a ride after she's just done me a huge favor. She has a used Volkswagen, but when I look out front where it's always parked, I see Jake driving off in it. It's too far to walk and still get there in time. For a moment, I consider not going. But only for a moment.

In the garage, my faithful bike has a flat. I panic. I decide to take Jake's. Forbidden, but under the circumstances, he might understand.

I'm the only one to arrive by bicycle. I look for a place to park it where it won't get stolen, and where it won't be conspicuous. Carloads of girls are unloading at the curb, streaming into the house in one female blur. I realize these people know each other, had someone to call for a ride, someone to commiserate with on the way over. I lean Jake's bike against the back of the pool house, and there is no one in the pool or the backyard. I walk around to the front and someone lets me in.

The room is full of girls I don't know, though many of the ones my age are familiar. There are two obvious groups—them and us. They are the members, older and already in the sorority. They all wear matching dresses, light blue with big white collars where matching blue Theta Rho letters are sewn on. We are those being rushed, our clothes varied, our swimsuits underneath. I recognize two cheerleaders from our junior high, now going into high school like me. They have no reason to speak to me and don't. Some girls I know from Honor Society. They are smart and popular; I am only smart. There is a difference. Jackie Lansing is on the other side of the room, eating a cracker with cheese. We were friends in seventh grade until we had a big fight and we haven't spoken since. Excuse me, excuse me, girls say as they politely move across the room through the crowd, to and from the food table. They seem like they've all been best friends forever. *BETSY, it is so good to SEE you!*

I sit alone on a velveteen love seat, light blue, Theta Rho color. I drink a champagne glass full of limeade that someone handed to me. Because I have no one to talk to, I look out the sliding glass doors to the pool beyond. The girl's father is scooping things out with a long net. A beetle, a roach, a drowning wasp.

I look back at Jackie Lansing, the only person I can imagine talking to, and thank God, she's looking at me. I smile. She makes the move through the room, toward where I sit, and I lose her temporarily in the throng, the blue and white.

"Hi," she says, "I like your outfit." She sits next to me on the love seat.

"It's my sister's. Thanks," I say.

"When did you find out you were going to be rushed?"

"Last week," I say.

"I've known all summer," Jackie says. "Lizzie, the president, she goes to my church. She got me in. I'm so nervous, are you?

"Yes," I say.

"They're going to ask us questions, like a personal interview," Jackie says.

I can't think of what they might ask, didn't know this would be so involved or so mysterious.

"Lizzie's told me a lot," Jackie says. "In fact, I heard this one thing..." She pauses. "No, I shouldn't tell you."

"What?" I say.

"It might just be a rumor, anyway," Jackie says.

"About what?"

"Okay. But don't tell anyone that I'm the one who told you," Jackie says. "I heard they're only rushing you because of Jake."

I shrug my shoulders.

"Do you think it's true?" Jackie says.

As we talk, something flows out of me onto my bathing suit. Thick and warm. The sensation is familiar and I am instantly panicked. I have nothing with me. I remember the blue velveteen and stand up. It is clean, still blue. "I'll be back," I say to Jackie, and I work my way through the crowd. "Excuse me, excuse me," I say.

"You're not serious," a girl is saying to a friend. Pieces of conversations. "Barb, you didn't!"

"I did. I am not joking!"

"Get out of here," someone says. Laughter. The smell of shampoo.

At the edge of the crowd, I come up for air. "Excuse me," I say again. I see a bathroom near the bottom of the staircase, slip inside, and close the door.

The din of girlish chatter is muffled by a fan that comes on with the light. Everything is clean and a coral color—sink, toilet, towels, and tiny soaps in shell shapes. I open the cabinet under the sink, where in our house the female paraphernalia is kept. Nothing. Ajax. More toilet paper. There are no other cupboards. I bleed into the toilet.

The bottoms of my bikini are already stained a deep red, it spreads through the fabric like ink. I wipe at the stain with a wad of Kleenex, first on one side, then the other. I drip into the coral bowl. The blood separates into the water, dilutes. I wet a Kleenex in the sink and dab again at the stain on my green suit. A knock comes on the door.

"Just a second," I say.

A voice says, "We're ready to start out here."

I stack four tissues and fold them over once, then again, making a pad. Carefully, I place this over the wet and smeared stain. I pull up the bottoms of my suit, checking to make sure the pad is in place. I feel the first drop ooze out onto the tissues. I flush and watch the evidence swirl until it disappears.

We are lined up on the stairs, two to a step. There must be thirty of us and as many of them. We are told we may talk quietly until it is our turn. They are all in the dining room and they call us in, pair by pair. Two girls at a time leave, and we all descend a step. They close the double doors and we speculate about what happens behind them. We cannot hear above our collective whisper. Information filters up and down the stairs. If even one member doesn't like you, you're out. Last year, three girls were blackballed from rush. During Hell Week, you can't even wash your hair.

I am relieved that I only sit on each step for a few minutes, then move down. I sit lightly and lean back. I am not in one place long enough to leave a trace. The carpet on the stairs is a creamy pile.

Jackie is my partner in this; she chose me when they said to get in twos. Now, though, she talks to the girls in front of us. Together, they conclude that the girls, who don't return to where we are, have been let out through the back, to the pool.

They compare stories of what they know, what they've heard. Jackie tells the worst story. That during Hell Night, you have to do something terrible with a pickle. "What?" someone asks, though we are all starting to imagine.

"They make you cram it," Jackie says.

Our mouths open.

"And that's not all," she says. "Then," she says, "they make you eat it."

We move down a step, then another, and the blood seeps into the Kleenex. I check each step that I leave. We have made it to the bottom step; Jackie wishes the girls in front of us luck.

In my ears, there's a distant roar like the ocean in a shell. We walk into the room. They are seated in folding chairs, all over the room. They line the edges; they sit around a big table, on the big table, next to the big table. An audience, a panel, uniformed blue and white. Their faces all look the same. We are told to stand in one spot.

Lizzie smiles at Jackie. "Don't be nervous," she says, and she tells us to speak about ourselves.

I tell them my favorite subject is English, that I sing, and want to learn guitar. I have a brother and a sister and my father is a doctor and my brother, he runs track.

Jackie goes after me and I don't hear what she says, because the ocean is still crashing in my ears.

"We want to ask you a question," Lizzie says, "and you should think hard about your answer. What does sorority mean to you?"

"It is a club of girls," I say. "They are all friends; they do things together." A stupid, pitiful answer, but I can think of nothing else. It is a nightmare, I could say, a horror, an embarrassment. More blood comes out, heavier, a gush, and I know the tissues are saturated. Jackie's answering now and I can't hear what she says.

We are lectured on the question, what our answers should

have been. What sorority really means. We are welcomed to rush, and invited to the next event which will be a pizza party at Shakey's. We are let out through the glass doors to the pool.

I am now leaking onto the shorts, Laura's shorts. I remove them by the pool house, and roll them into a tight ball. I slip into the deep end, where the water is darker. I move my legs in a kicking motion. Some girls do fancy dives off the board. I stay out of their way, pretend I am there to watch, keep my legs moving, the water circulating.

I remember a time when I was little, and taking a bath with Laura. Laura was nine. I peed in the water—it was the warmth and the wet that made me do it. Laura stood up, shocked. "You think I can't see what you did?" she said, and I looked down to see the yellow coming out of me, darker at the source, blending slowly into clear.

I move to the other side of the pool, try to spread myself thin. I keep my legs moving, as I alternately tread water or hang onto the side. Girls grow in clusters around tables with umbrellas. Several line the steps in the shallow end, like a beauty pageant swimsuit competition. Some girls don't get their hair wet. The members come out of the house finally, still in their dresses, they don't swim. They mill around, passing food and filling cups. They make easy conversation. I thrash around in the deep end, and feel like I have been doing this for an hour. Hoisting myself out, I sit on the side. A puddle forms beneath me, tinged with pink. I splash water from the pool to wash it away. I grab Laura's shorts and put them on, wet as I am. I walk over to where Jackie dangles her feet in the shallow end, and tell her I'm leaving.

She tells me it's too early. "The party isn't over. It won't look good," she says.

"I have to be somewhere," I tell her, and shrug, like it's out of my control. I don't say good-bye to anyone else.

Outside the gate, I am trembling as I get on Jake's bike. The vinyl cover on his seat is torn halfway off, exposing yellowish foam underneath. I bleed on this seat. All the way home, it seeps out of me. Tinted water runs in streams down my legs.

Sisterhood was the correct answer to the question they asked. Jackie and I both got it wrong. Sorority means sisterhood. "If you get in," they said, "if you make it, all of us will be like sisters to you. It is not a club, but much, much more."

I pass up my house and go straight to Izzy's. She answers the door; she expects me. "What's wrong?" she says, and I tell her.

In their bathroom, I know where the tampons are. The wad of Kleenex is shredded and soaked; I dispose of it. We go in her room and she gives me some clothes, and she wraps the wet ones in a towel.

"Isn't this Laura's?" she says.

I nod.

"Oh, God," she says.

While the clothes are spinning in Izzy's mother's washer, we go out and move the bike to the backyard. I press down on the seat with two fingers; a puddle of watery blood fills the indentation. Izzy says wait and unrolls the hose from the side of the house. We spray the seat hard, press down on the foam, spray again.

"Were they nice?" Izzy says.

"Not especially."

"You couldn't ask someone for a tampon?"

"No."

We continue washing down the seat of the bike, squeezing it like a sponge.

"So, what's next?" Izzy says.

"Pizza party. On Friday."

"You'll go?"

I stop what I'm doing and stand there and realize that until Izzy just said that, I didn't remember I had a choice. She's holding the hose, waiting for me to answer. I could just *not go*. I could blackball myself. Save myself a lot of misery.

Izzy says, "Well, anyway, you have a week to think about it."
"I don't need a week," I say. And then I smile. "No way I'm going." And she smiles back

Izzy takes a long drink from the hose, and then passes it to me. I drink and then turn it off, while Izzy wraps a dry towel around the bicycle seat, pressing the water out. She parks Jake's bike in the sun.

"It's clean," she says, and I follow her inside where she puts my clothes in the dryer.

Siobhan Dowd, program director of PEN American Center's Freedom-to-Write Committee, writes this column regularly, alerting readers to the plight of writers around the world who deserve our awareness and our writing action.

Silenced Voice: Ali-Akbar Saidi-Sirjani
by Siobhan Dowd

*J*t is easier for me to die by injustice than to acquiesce to it." So wrote Ali-Akbar Saidi-Sirjani, one of Iran's most celebrated authors, to Iran's spiritual ruler, the Ayatollah Khamenei. Three years later, Saidi-Sirjani's words have come to seem sadly prescient: he is currently in prison and in grave danger of facing a death sentence.

There has been much speculation as to why Saidi-Sirjani was arrested last March. The official press has claimed that he has confessed and is to be tried for drug trafficking, sodomy, and receiving money from "counterrevolution-

Ali-Akbar Saidi-Sirjani

ary" associations abroad, all of which charges carry the death penalty. His friends, however, believe that the real reason for his arrest lies in his satirical writings and his criticism of certain aspects of the Iranian Revolution.

Still others believe that the case cannot be separated from the tragic suicide of Professor Homa Darabi: Three weeks before Saidi-Sirjani's arrest, Darabi, after being dismissed from her job at the University of Tehran for failing to wear the correct hejab (head covering), poured kerosene over herself, shouted "Long live freedom!" and burned herself alive in a busy city square. The incident profoundly shocked the country, and the authorities quickly moved to prevent all discussion of it in the press. They also, it is conjectured, feared Saidi-Sirjani's reaction to the affair, given his immense popularity in Iran and his long record of acerbic criticism of intolerance. His sudden arrest may have been aimed at ensuring his silence.

Whatever the reasons for Saidi-Sirjani's detention, the fact that he is in grave danger is undisputed. Friends believe that the charges are trumped up, and that the tone of the official newspapers bodes badly, as does the recent staging of a demonstration outside a government office during which a pro-government mob demanded Saidi-Sirjani's execution.

Saidi-Sirjani, sixty-three, is married, with three children. One of his friends, who asked to remain anonymous, has described him as a "distinguished man of letters, writer, essayist, and social critic with a great reputation both in Persia and abroad, not only for his social criticism, his inimitable style, and his biting humor, but also for his abundant courage." Over the years, Saidi-Sirjani has poured his literary scorn equally on the shah and the Islamic Republic, although he apparently welcomed the greater liberality President Rafsanjani seemed to promise on first coming to office.

In 1987, he was a visiting professor in Persian literature at Columbia University in New York and, while there, he contributed scholarly articles to works such as the *Encyclopedia Iranica*. He is also the author of several best-selling books, including the novella *Zahak-e-Mardoosh (Zahak, the Snake Man)*, a recasting of a mythical tale from the Persian national epic, the

Shanama, or *Book of Kings.* He has lived chiefly in Tehran, where, despite increasingly vicious attacks on him in the official press, he has continued to publish critical essays and literary allegories with strong social implications. Some of his books have sold up to fifty thousand copies—ten times more than the print run for most titles in Iran.

In recent years, however, Saidi-Sirjani's books have been in effect banned by the Ministry of Culture and Islamic Guidance, which has refused to grant his publishers the necessary permits for their distribution. Saidi-Sirjani's frustration at this move led him to write scathing letters about Iranian censorship to friends abroad, and to attempt to distribute his books himself.

Saidi-Sirjani's March 14 arrest occurred while he was leaving a friend's house accompanied by Niazi-Kermani, a publisher and poet. Both he and Niazi-Kermani were taken to a place of detention that has yet to be disclosed. Later that day, agents of the anti-vice department of the Revolutionary Prosecutor's Office raided his home, seizing his papers and searching and then sealing off his library.

News of Saidi-Sirjani's reported "confession" appeared some five weeks later in the newspaper *Jomhuri Eslami.* The Director-General of National Security at the Ministry of Intelligence was reported to have stated that both men had confessed to repeated acts of sodomy, drug trafficking, contacts with former agents of the shah's secret-police service, and receiving money from abroad. In fact, Saidi-Sirjani frequently refused money from foreign organizations, including a recent Hellman/Hammett Award granted by the Human Rights Watch's Free Expression Project. As for the other charges, many experts on Iran point out that the accusation of espionage activities is a standard mechanism for dealing with dissent.

Saidi-Sirjani's wife is reportedly devastated by the newspaper's claims. She has said publicly that, in thirty years of marriage, she never detected any such traits in her husband. Saidi-Sirjani himself, however, seems all along to have fully appreciated that his vocal opposition to the government might result in his death, notwithstanding the protection his immense popularity has afforded him in the past. In his open letter to the Ayatollah Khamenei, he wrote:

> This is probably my last letter to you, as I sincerely look forward to the final call from my creator. There is nothing in this world to make me wish to stay. Please go ahead and have me arrested and killed for the crimes that have been fabricated in my name—or else listen to my call for justice and explain to me why my books are censored.

Please write courteous letters, urging that the reported charges being pressed against Ali-Akbar Saidi-Sirjani do not merit the death penalty and requesting his release to:

His Excellency Ali-Akbar Hashemi Rafsanjani
The Presidency
Palestine Avenue
Azerbaijan Intersection
Tehran
ISLAMIC REPUBLIC OF IRAN

Monica Wood

*This is me in 1953 with my mother, my sister Betty, and my
grandmother lurking in the background. I don't know why I look so
worried; my mother was an angel. To this day, I love baths.
P.S. They called me Pumpkinhead for a reason.*

Monica Wood is the author of the novel *Secret Language* (Faber and Faber,
1993); the forthcoming writing manual *Description* (Writer's Digest Books);
the editor of *Short Takes: 15 Contemporary Stories* (J. Weston Walch, 1992); and
the author of numerous short stories that have appeared in a variety of
magazines, most recently *Redbook, North American Review,* and *Manoa.* Her
stories have been nominated three times for the National Magazine Awards
and the Pushcart Prize (special mention, 1991), frequently anthologized, and
featured on American Public Radio. Currently, she is at work on a second
novel, tentatively titled *The Family Official,* and she has just completed a full-
length play, titled *Contrition.*

A Maine native, Wood is a free-lance copy editor who teaches fiction writing
part-time for the USM Department of Community Programs in Portland,
Maine, where she has lived for seventeen years.

Monica Wood

MONICA WOOD

A Ghost Story

I

t's the children I see first, sometimes whole legions of
them in high button shoes that fade as they touch the floor. You
think the souls of children depart in an instant, freed from the
temporal world? Think again. Like those tortured creatures
dragging their chains across the floorboards of an attic, children
have intentions, too. Amends and reminders. Old business.
Sometimes they stay to comfort their mothers, then hang around
for generations out of habit. Or maybe they're bound to the
earth by handed-down grief: Some families are like that, sad over
they don't know what, possessed of downward-curving mouths
and soulful, wide-set eyes, unconscious of that coal of memory,
decades or centuries old, lodged in their roiling guts.

Most often, though (others disagree but this has been my
experience), the children stay simply because they're curious;
they refuse to vacate the premises in case they might hear
something interesting. About Christmas coming, or a sick
grandmother, or the neighbor dog's new puppies. Generations
pass, centuries, and our stories still have the power to thrill them.
Kids.

Women inhabit these places, too, stripped of their earthly
gifts, their features dry and silvery, nearly translucent. Gone is
their precise beauty, no hint of race or station, no flesh or bone

or coil of hair, nothing you'd care to call texture. They're like
curtains floating on a breeze, tatters of light. Sometimes—rarely,
I've found—you can determine the flutter of an eyelid, the
general impression of a corpus.

The men who stay on are your oddballs—murdered horse
thieves bent on revenge; twin brothers who lost the farm. Not
many, though; one in twenty. In my experience men leave this
earth believing they owe nothing, and the ones who stay are set
only on retrieving their possessions.

Like most people, Andrew shies from my vocation, but then
he's wrestling his own ghosts. I've known him long enough so
I remember how he was before his wife and sons died. We had
twelve in the department then; it was like running an orphanage,
they were all such babies. I liked Andrew, though. I liked his
earnest befuddlement; it came from being so enormously loved.
He never had to worry about his little place in this world. The
others stalked my desk with sheaves of paper that made up the
dense and tedious little articles they placed atop my "in" box,
squaring the pages just so. Andrew, on the other hand, was the
day-late, dollar-short type, always apologizing, no hurry, no
hurry, his feathery pages landing on my desk like a bird's nest
dropped out of a tree. He was the only one who noticed that I
could type a bibliography without looking at a stylebook. Who
thanked me for it. I charged his wife with these gifts. Really, his
wife was a doll.

Nowadays he's sharp and vigilant; his eyes have lost the
dreamy look of comfort. He marks the end of a day with a check
on the calendar, as if twenty-four hours safely passed is a little
victory. I suppose it is.

I came to my vocation right here in the English department.
Actually, we were on the sunny third floor of Martin Hall then,
long before the cutbacks and whatnot, before they stashed us in
this dungeon and the underside of everybody's personality came

slithering out. This was way back, in the days when the university still ran courses like "Secrets of the Tarot," when the Adult Ed department was anything-goes. This was before certain alumni and department heads got testy—for some reason all these courses were held in Martin, and the English department was afraid of reputation by association. Eventually, the trustees heaved all the good stuff from the course guide. I miss those courses, miss watching the retired mailmen and middle-aged mothers tripping down the hall toward Sam Collins's lecture hall, brand-new notebooks clutched to their waists.

It was a spring day, tart and promising, when I took it into my head to sit in on one of those lectures. Yvette—the secretary of the history department, two doors down from us—had been going for weeks. She liked to stop at my door on her way back to the office to give me the blow-by-blow: auras, spoon-bending, spirit-writing.

I popped into Andrew's office. "I'm taking lunch early, in case anybody wants me." He was buried in test papers, his burnished, hairy forearms resting over the exams like outsized paper-weights. He looked stranded there, almost bereft, though it was a familiar enough scene, a professor at his desk. Dare I say I had a premonition? I felt a curious empty space, that stopped-moment feeling you get just before the car hits the wall. This was seven years ago; his wife and sons would be dead within the year, a spectacular car crash with lots of noise and light. But I'm not telepathic. I see ghosts, and that's another sensitivity altogether.

I tapped on Andrew's desk to shake off the feeling. "I'm going to hear Sam Collins," I told him.

He looked up. "You're joking."

"You teach Irish lit, Andrew. Don't you believe in ghosts?"

"Well," he said. "No."

"He's no quack, Andrew. He's known all over. Remember that house in the paper last year, the one with the weeping widow? That was him."

Andrew smiled. "Rusty's into ghosts these days. Must be the age." Rusty was the younger son, the one who survived sixty-two hours.

Next thing I knew he was sauntering down the hall with me, admiring the auburn glint of sunlight banking through the windows of Martin Hall's east side. "I don't get out enough," he said, though in truth he got out a lot back then, to watch his sons play ball in grassy pastures, to stroll the spring-blooming campus with his wife. He rarely wore a jacket and never wore a hat, not even in winter when his ears flamed at the tips. These days he dresses too warm, his raincoats and fleece-lined jackets and wool caps and kidskin gloves a submission to our climate's capricious changes. Sometimes I think he's afraid of air itself.

On this day, however, he was dressed in short sleeves that flapped against his elbows as we headed down the hall. All of a sudden I felt we were in for a shot of whimsy, something we could take home that night to our respective houses, a bit of glitter we might spread around. I could imagine the stilled faces of his wife and sons, listening to Andrew's fabulous story. I felt light and floaty. That weightless feeling was the first feeble stirring of love, though I only know that now.

We got there about halfway through the presentation. Sam Collins wasn't above milking his hype: He wore some sort of woolen cloak and he'd lined his eyes in black, making the blue that much more piercing. I could never do that. On the table next to him was a deck of cards, some silver spoons, a tape recorder, some blown-up photographs of spooky-looking mansions. Dog-and-pony show, I thought, my brief belief in whimsy dried up and gone, just like that. As I moved to leave he called Andrew to the front of the room.

Andrew played the amiable professor, which amused the five or six of his own students who dotted the crowd of eccentrics and housewives. He dawdled up the center aisle, extravagantly calm, trying to avoid the thin blue lasers of Sam's made-up eyes.

"How do you do," Sam said. "Have a seat." Andrew sat. I watched him flinch as Sam's hand fluttered down to his shoulder and balanced there. "We've been talking about color," Sam began. He was looking out at the students, but his hand remained where it was. He was getting a reading on Andrew, though you wouldn't have known it, his eyes darting everywhere. "Colors are mirrors," he announced. "For example, I can tell you something about the past twenty-four hours of this man's life simply by the colors he chose to wear today."

I shifted in my chair, suddenly more interested than I had expected to be.

"Your name?" Sam said.

"Andrew."

"Andrew, you're wearing a lot of hidden red." Andrew cleared his throat, mortified. Sam was now moving through the rows, arching his long, thin fingers through the air. "His tie looks navy from a distance, but up close you can see a pattern of red diamonds. His socks? Same thing. And what's that peering out of his breast pocket? Four pens, red caps." Sam halted midway to the back of the room. He folded his hands. "Red is anger," he told the class. "Andrew had a bad day yesterday. His clothing today tells the tale."

Andrew's mouth actually opened, that's how stunned, or something, he was. I think I might have covered my face, though I remember the look he flashed me.

Then Sam turned to me. "Green," he went on, "is serenity. This woman in the green dress—yesterday was a good day for you, yes?"

"Yes," I said. "But all my days are good, really. Green's my favorite color."

He continued on, touching down on one student after another. Somehow, Andrew got back to his seat unnoticed. When the class broke up he left swiftly, and before I could go after him I felt the heat of Sam's hand on my own shoulder.

"Wait," he said. "I'd like to ask you some questions." That was the beginning of my training.

I didn't get back to the office for another hour. Andrew was still grading papers. "I'm sorry," I told him. "I had no idea he'd be so, um, rude."

He grimaced and took my hand. His cool skin was a surprise. "The man was right," he said. You work with a guy for years and think you know his every mood. This one I had never seen: It was trouble of the broken-heart variety. I could have cried on the spot.

"Thank you," he said, "for having only good days."

"They're not all good," I said. "Just most of them." I took back my hand and fled to my desk, as if apologizing for being happy.

They say marriages have highs and lows. I wouldn't know, but I've always wondered if she had taken a lover, something like that. In any case, they made up. Eventually he returned to his old, loved self. And stayed that way. Then she died.

Andrew and I don't have what you'd call a torrid relationship. I could see being married to him, though. I could see waking to his face in the morning across our frumped-up double bed. Yvette says the man is poison, in love with a ghost, a lost cause. If you ever want to be happy, Yvette says, you better look around for someone a little more willing to start over.

I've had two lovers in forty years, counting Andrew. I've always been self-conscious about my weight and I suppose that's hindered me somewhat in the romantic arena, but truth be told I'm not a very sexual person. I'm not one of those people who thinks sex is satin sheets and *Bolero* on the radio; I guess you could say my energies are channeled elsewhere. Andrew is fifty-three years old, a fact he reminds me of often. It's supposed to mean he's too old for something—for life, I guess—though he's never said exactly what. In bed, he's sweet; he talks to me. We could be playing Scrabble or skipping rocks at the beach; it's quiet like that. Andrew possesses the kind of soul that will linger on the earth for a few years to warm some young couple's house, to turn the iron off if they forget to, to sit up all night in the nursery with the baby they never believed they'd have.

When I finally fell in love with Andrew I was deep into my vocation, having finished my training and roamed a few houses on my own. I'd gotten a disgruntled colonist to vacate the Van Buren place in Standish. And I had determined that the nocturnal wall-scratching at the Goldings' was nothing more diabolical than a family of squirrels. I hadn't wanted my extracurricular activities to get around the office, of course, but with Yvette two doors down you could just forget it.

I was clearing my desk at the end of the day when Andrew wandered into the office after teaching his Joyce class. I opened my bottom drawer and handed back his copy of *Ulysses*, setting it on top of the stack of student papers he had bunched in his arms.

"You read it?" he asked.

"Every inch." He'd given me the book on a dare, trying to break me from my romance-novel habit, which, I'll admit, was a guilty pleasure.

"And?"

I flicked my fingers at the book. "And, I think I get it."

He tried to smile. It had been four years since the accident, and the corners of his mouth were more or less permanently turned down, but there was still something behind his eyes, a spark of life. "Let's hear it," he said.

"For your information," I said, "this book wasn't written to be understood. That's why nobody understands it." I lifted my chin toward the papers. "Those poor kids." Andrew began to chuckle, his blue eyes darkening under those wiry eyebrows. I remember thinking that he was kind of handsome. "It's a hoax," I continued. "Joyce's sole intention was to tongue-tie well-meaning scholars like you for generations to come."

He laughed out loud then—such a spangled, foreign sound, a silvery gift. Al Washington, who was strolling out of his office, stopped to stare. It had been so long since any of us had heard Andrew laugh.

Al thumped an unfootnoted, hundred-pound manuscript on my desk. "Molly's deconstructing Joyce, is she?"

Andrew nodded, smiling. "An interesting theory, however unprovable."

"How's the ghost-busting?" Al asked.

I crossed my arms and looked at him. "You won't think it's so funny when your windows start opening themselves."

"You should make those ding-dongs pay you," Al said. "This little hobby of yours is a gold mine and you don't even know it." He laid his hand on the manuscript. "By next Friday?" he said, then left for a class.

"They don't pay you?" Andrew said.

"Who?"

"Those people. Who think they have ghosts in their walls."

"I don't ask them to." I was driven then, as now, by other desires: connection, mainly.

"Work is worth money," Andrew said. "I wouldn't teach for free, much as I love it."

"They pay my transportation if I need it," I explained. "They put me up in a hotel if I have to stay a few days."

"They should pay you for your work, Molly," Andrew said. "Your vocation is worth something to those people."

I believe that was our beginning. "Vocation" is a beautiful word.

All this is to say that after almost two years of being a couple, or whatever it is we are, Andrew agreed to go on an investigation with me. I can understand his reluctance; he associates ghosts with death. Most people do. It's their life that makes them interesting to me, though. It's their life that allows me to see them.

I was after him all last week, tempting him with bits of information about the Coopers and their two-hundred-year-old farmhouse hours from here, deep in the country. The man works in a paper mill; the woman stays home with their retarded daughter. They grow beets and beans and pumpkins. Finally, last night, Andrew said yes.

If I've neglected to say so, let me say it now: Most of these people are lying. They take their private rages against each other or themselves and turn it into footsteps in the night. Nine times out of ten they're on the brink of divorce and don't know it, or else one of the kids abused his sister and hasn't yet fessed up. Ugly stuff. It's all very sophisticated, all to do with mysteries of the human heart that I can't begin to measure, but Sam warned me to watch for them, the ones who get mad at you for not hearing what they hear. Every once in a while I'll call up Sam—he's mostly retired now—and we nod at either end of the phone. Yes, isn't it the truth, the walls really do have ears, and voices, too. We call them "echoes," made-up phantoms that mimic your most private fears. I've seen it a hundred times. Help us, they say, the whole family. Help us, we can't live here anymore; we can't stand it. Well, they're right, but it has nothing to do with a ghost.

I've asked Andrew to drive, hoping to distract him. Even the most diehard of skeptics get nervous around allegedly haunted houses. Not that Andrew is a diehard, or a skeptic. He's shrouded, is all. Shrouded in his own grief, ticking off one minute after the other, marking his distance from loss. He stays with me because I allow him to come in and out of his stupor, to be near or far whenever he has to be. I'm patient. I've been waiting, in one way or another, all my life. Sam says it's my greatest virtue; he saw it that day I wore green. When we walked into that first house together and I said, "I see them," he wasn't even surprised.

This afternoon Andrew keeps looking at me as he drives, the final shadows of daylight silking across his face, or what I can see of it. Even in the car, which has a good heater, he keeps his hat pulled down, his scarf cinched at the neck. "I've been counting," he says. "It's been nearly two years for us, Molly." He lowers his face, frowning, his chin disappearing into his scarf. "A lot of women would have expected something by now. Demanded something."

"I'm not a lot of women."

He glances back at the road. "That's true."

"Turn here," I tell him.

"You know I couldn't get married again," he murmurs, swinging the car wide around the border of a frost-crisped field. "I couldn't have any more children. You have a right to those things."

"That's just Yvette. Don't listen to her. She thinks she knows everything."

"Still, I wouldn't blame you, Molly."

"I'm happy," I tell him. I reach across the seat and feel under his scarf to knead the back of his neck.

"But you're a young woman still," he says. He keeps swallowing dryly, dispensing the words a few at a time. "You could still have a husband and babies, all those things."

"I want you, Andrew. Just like this."

He sighs. "Thank you." We drive on, a mile, two, along acres of snow-dusted fields.

The Cooper place turns out to be a bit nicer than I imagined. New paint, a red and stolid barn, a tidy stand of pines separating the house from the field. All the signs of a sturdy family. We get out of the car and stand for a moment in the dooryard, watching the daylight disappear on the landscape. The farthest trees are quivering ominously, and I can hear the faint whining of a far-off winter wind.

"Damn this weather," Andrew mutters, sounding like an old man. "Yesterday it could've been spring."

Mrs. Cooper meets us at the door. She's a tall, lean woman in a cotton shirt and blue jeans, her hair pulled back from her face except for a few dozen loose strands that define her hairline. A nice woman, unsentimental, willing to tell the truth. I believe her already. Her little daughter stands just behind her, arms twined 'round her mother's waist, hands clasped in a bow at the center of her mother's belt. "My husband's not back from work yet," Mrs. Cooper says. She covers her little girl's hands with her own. "This is Sheila. She's been awfully frightened." She lifts one hand and wipes her hair back from her forehead. "She's very sensitive to noise, and this—this *clattering*—up and down the stairs, sometimes four, five times in a day."

"May we come in?" I ask.

"Oh, I'm sorry, of course." Mrs. Cooper steps aside. I introduce Andrew, who isn't paying attention; he's watching the little girl. She might be smiling, though it's hard to tell: her face is a trifle lopsided, the eyes nearly crossed, all the features askew in some unnameable way. Andrew reaches into his pocket and withdraws a marble, a blue cat's-eye. I suddenly remember Andrew the way he was a long time ago, joking that his kids only loved him for his pockets.

Sheila makes a joyful gurgling sound and tears upstairs. Mrs. Cooper laughs. "You've got her number already. She collects everything." We sit at the dining room table, a big, old-fashioned thing with drawers. Already I can see them, two children, their features obscured by light, their small bodies undulating like milky water. They appear to be girls, hovering near the ancient hearth, listening.

"Now," I begin, pulling my tape recorder out of my satchel. "Does this presence do anything else besides run up and down the stairs?"

Mrs. Cooper frowns, thinking. The children huddle together,

covering their mouths. I think they're laughing.

"Do you feel you're in any danger?" Andrew asks. I turn to him, startled. His face is devoid of motion; it's like looking at a statue of Andrew in a museum.

"No," Mrs. Cooper stammers. "No, not really. It's just that the noise scares Sheila." She knits her fingers together for a moment, then looks up, embarrassed. "I think the—the spirits or whatever—have been leaving me presents."

I can't help smiling; I've seen this before. "Can you show me?" I ask, and just then Sheila reappears and opens the dining-table drawer herself, extracting a fistful of leaves. She makes a thin, guttural sound and gives them to Andrew.

"Leaves," he says.

"And pins," Mrs. Cooper whispers, her eyes large and curious, "and knotted lengths of twine, and buttons from my sewing basket. Nearly every morning there's something at my place at the table."

"You're a mother," I tell her gently. "The spirits are children." Mrs. Cooper spreads one hand over her chest. "I thought they might be," she murmurs. "How many?"

I glance at Andrew to see how he's taking this. He's waxen and still, his head cocked at an angle. He looks startlingly old, frozen that way. "Two," I say. "They're standing right over there."

Mrs. Cooper looks at the hearth for a long time, then back at me. She squeezes her hands together in a prayer. "Are they beautiful?"

"Yes."

"I'm so glad," she says, then wraps her imperfect, living daughter in her arms.

By the time we leave it has gotten dark and gusty; the moonlit, snowed-on fields seem like an endless ripple of broken glass. "Where did you come up with the marble?" I ask Andrew.

His face is fixed on the road. "I keep it for luck."

We don't speak for miles. Finally, I begin: "The next step is usually to ransack the library and town hall for records. Census, land transfers, things like that. If I can figure out who the children are, I've got a better chance of getting them to leave."

"Why would she want them to leave?" Andrew slows the car down and eases it to the side of the road.

"What are you doing?"

"I need—air," he gasps, then flings the door open and steps onto the road. Before I know it, he's moving alongside the sugary fields like a farmer walking his acreage.

"Andrew?" I call, getting out. The windy cold is a bright slap; I stop to catch my breath. "Andrew?" He's sitting now, yards away. Sitting on the side of the road. His hat is gone, upended in a sudden gust and tumbling across the asphalt. His hair stands up in silvery tufts. I hurry to him, my shoes making sparks of sound on the frozen shoulder.

He looks up at me. "I saw them," he says.

"You saw—"

"The children. By the hearth." He's crying now, big, muddy, man-sized sobs.

"Andrew, oh." I crouch down to see him. "Oh, sweetheart. It's all right."

He cannot be consoled. I remember this feeling—wonderment, terror, chagrin. I cried too, as I recall. But, of course, there's more here.

"They haven't left you, Andrew," I tell him. "They'll never leave you, no matter what you do." And that's when I see it, a thin shred of light wound around his trouser leg like the silky arms of a child.

"I'm fifty-three years old," Andrew whispers.

"Yes, I know."

"I've walked this earth fifty-three years."

"Yes."

"I've seen things a man shouldn't see." He's speaking of their bloodless, laid-out bodies festooned with flowers, their hair combed just slightly wrong by a mortician's assistant. "Still..." he begins. The light around his leg is dissolving now, a starry shimmer, like a fireworks disintegrating against a black sky. I have to swallow a couple of times, it's so beautiful.

I clasp his hand. "Still."

He nods and looks up at the moon, his face dropping years in the icy light. "You hear that?" he asks.

We fall silent and listen. From far down the crystalled land comes a wild whooshing, a magnificent gust of Canadian air winding across the field. His arm comes around and I hide in his shelter as the tenor of wind swells, gushing over fences and barns and phone poles and curves of road. It is a huge, benevolent, rushing sound, a great, earthly straining, and he raises his head to meet it, his pale neck bared above his loosened scarf: a sound like the shedding of trees, like the parting of water, like the opening of a man's hobbled heart.

A Woman, Three Novels, a Muse, and a Bear
An essay by Joyce Thompson

I

I write this on a damp and pearl gray February morning.

Across the sound, the mist lifts from beneath, so a ghost of the city on the opposite shore is shiftingly visible under a white mass of dense, quilt-stuffing clouds. The computer hums steadily, the space heater, intermittently. With the persistent irregularity of a faucet left barely open to keep the pipes from freezing on a winter night, rain drips from a hole in the porch roof into the growing puddle below. Down on the beach, fifty feet from my open window, a lazy gray low tide licks the sand. Both the freighter that takes shape out of the mist as it finds the channel and the gulls drifting in the windless moist air are silent as they come. Small, local music, a landscape whose shifts are as slow and mysteriously purposeful as a tai chi master doing the form at dawn, a time and place so distant from the world's business I would mistake my life for a painting if it were not for the alternating currents of panic and hope that flash and surge inside me. I am aware, as I write this, how much I envy people whose days are shaped by the clear imperatives of clocks, appointments, jobs. I am aware, too, that some of them may envy me.

How did this moment come? Late in the Reagan years, I was

obsessed by darkness, felt a deep shadow I perceived to be evil afoot in the culture and in the world. Out of my fear, trying to face it down, I wrote a dark novel then, one whose process and imaginings drew me so deep into that darkness, brought me so close to the dark flame that burns there I emerged from the journey shaken and scorched, feeling sullied by my traffic with forces I had come to believe were not only real but beyond my understanding or control. This might not have happened if I were a different kind of writer, one who oversees a story more than she surrenders to it. It might not have happened if real life had not cast up an ugly and terrifying series of events that coincided so frighteningly with the fiction I was writing. But so life did.

Even as I wrote the chapter which put a fictional child in mortal jeopardy, my best friend's real one was found dead. The years of labor I had put into that work ended in mourning and a sense of guilt the passage of four years has not assuaged. Worse yet, since I had a family to support, two children of my own to feed and a contractual obligation to discharge, the tainted thing I had made could not be buried or disowned but had to undergo the inevitable transformation into an article of commerce, something to be published, packaged, hyped, and sold. Its proprietors were delighted by how horrifying the story was, how real it seemed. The Book of the Month Club gave it a label— Mystery. The publisher, to whom I owed another novel, demanded another mystery. I was heartsick and ashamed. I did not want to go back into the darkness.

There are a lot of truths I would find easier than these to tell— my weight, my age, the particulars of my sex life, such as it is— all those conventional secrets feel far less intimate than the odd psychic progress of my writing life, less foolish and less shameful. In the middle of the last dark weeks of writing my last dark novel, one hopeful small thing happened. Wanting to relax and replenish myself a bit and to reward my children for their patience, I took them on a weekend trip to see the fields of tulips that open in the Skagit Valley every springtime. The weather was moody, mostly gray, and the fields muddy, but the blooming was prodigious, bright, and extravagant. We bought ourselves flowers, ate out, saw a movie, stayed the night in a motel. On toward morning, with my son asleep beside me, I fell into a dream.

I held a book open in my hands, and, as I strained to read it, left to right and line by line the letters of the words turned into flowers. Slowly at first, then with increasing speed, the left-hand page became a garden. My eye tracked right, the words printed there blossomed, and at the right-hand margin of the right-hand page, the rows of blossoms scrolled up into a living pillar of flowers, white touched with pink. As I woke from that image, two words formed in my mind—*Paradise Illustrated*. Opening my eyes, raising up on one elbow, I thought, *I want to write a comic novel.*

It was a sweet dream, a little kindness of my psyche, and I felt happier that morning than I had for a long time. What puzzles and shames me, four years later, is how totally I embraced that sliver of light, how tightly I have held those flowers, how unquestioningly I accepted a few moments' dreaming as a direction for my life and work. Once before, a novel had come to me this way, arrived instead of rising up inside me, as if it were a gift of vision and conviction. That novel should have been beyond my skill, but the sense that I had not chosen but been assigned to write it gave me the tenacity and the humility to stretch and grow until I could. Both artistically and by the warmth and width of its reception, I knew it to be the best of my novels. That spring morning in La Conner, I was willing to believe I had received another assignment, and I was grateful.

I had to go home; I had to satisfy my pact with the devil and finish my dark book, but I carried the seed of something brighter in me and, through the next months, tended it. I reread

Essay: *A Woman, Three Novels, a Muse, and a Bear*

Shakespeare's comedies and a lot of comic novels, went back to Northrup Frye's *The Types of Literature*, and wallowed in the mythos of spring. Little by little, tendrils of character and the green shoots of story began to show forth, a wordless vision finding particular narrative form. I have always been entranced by metamorphosis, art's most potent metaphor and the only magic trick that nature does; nurturing my vision, I felt I was involved in something healthy and redemptive. When it came time to propose the next book to my editor, I knew enough about it to propose it eloquently. The human heart is a mystery, what we laugh at is mysterious, and how we find our faith— those were my arguments.

My editor said no. He said a mystery is full of fear and death. He said it was the only kind of book he would accept from me. "Write your comic novel if you must, but you still owe me a mystery."

So comes another shameful moment. My children and I had just moved into a small, unfinished beach cabin my father had built on summer weekends in the 1950s; the money the dark novel earned me had gone into patching walls to ceiling, painting, getting the wiring up to code, buying a woodstove to keep us warm in winter. My checking account was empty. In two days of long showers and long walks on the beach, I concocted an impossibly convoluted Gothic mystery plot and swore I could write it in first person. My editor sent me a check for the first half of the advance and I cashed it, vowing I would make art.

Eight sullen months later, I had two-thirds of a novel that was beautifully written and slower than snail spit, a maimed creation that was neither the thriller my editor wanted to publish nor the work of literature I wanted to write. I told myself then, and probably believe it still, that without the freedom to fail there can be no creativity. Money was tight and getting tighter, but I put the manuscript in the Dumpster, where it belonged. It was time to write my comic novel. I prayed it would come easy.

In the beginning, it did. A voice began to speak, and it spoke funny, even though what it chose to talk about was death, death and sex in the first paragraph. The sentences came easy and elegant, the paragraphs had rhythm, suspense, periodicity. The voice shocked and thrilled me with its humor and its clear-eyed callousness and, most of all, with its eagerness to keep on talking. It knew the story it had to tell. By the third chapter, it had shown itself capable, not just of honesty and wit, but of poignancy and a kind of dignity. I began to intuit that the voice's impiety, its edged humor, were a kind of armor against pain. The speaker was she, a woman. I did not recognize her as myself. For seven months, I—she—kept writing. We climbed a mountain and hit a snag.

A couple writing conferences and a couple stories saw us through the summer. It did not abet my work-passion that, for a while, I fell in love with a real-life man. That autumn I was confident enough the book would find its rightful ending that I borrowed living money from some friends. By early spring, I finished a first draft, but was not done a week before I realized it was not done right. Notes from the morning I started a second draft remind me I was grim and desperate and depressed. Had it not been for the mystical assignment, I would have chucked this one in the Dumpster, too, and been relieved; I longed to bitch out the Assigner, but didn't know whom, exactly, to curse. For something over two months of dogged daily work, I polished and recrafted the front end of the novel, right up to the place I'd gone astray before—the mountain. And the snag.

For the first time in a long and increasingly amicable estrangement, my former husband invited our children to spend half of the summer vacation with him, and I assented. In almost twenty years, I had not been alone for more than a long weekend; I had no sense of what shape my days would take without the wants and needs of others to be their template, or what my rhythms of living and working would turn out to be. I wondered if I would be lonely and, more urgently, if I could be disciplined.

When I first began writing novels, I had a capacity for work so natural and abiding that, while others called it discipline, it seemed more like simple appetite to me. The arrival of one child, then another, transformed appetite to struggle and writing to the occupation of those hours I could steal from parenting, householding, teaching, and sleep, bought from day-care providers, borrowed from relatives and friends. Each working session was circumscribed from the first minute by the knowledge of when it had to end; I feared that over time, my imagination, my concentration, my vision, and the flow of my prose had shrunk to accommodate that limitation. My chapters had grown shorter, my formal experiments fewer over time. To reread a novel I had written was to remember the interruptions, anticipated and unexpected, that had helped to shape the course of my stories.

Entering my six-week solitude, I knew myself to be less ambitious than I had been two decades before. I didn't know if this were the result of maturity—a tempering of ego, a shift of the reasons I want and need to write—or simply an erosion of my expectations, a giving up. While I've often had to ask my muse to work for money, to amass a fortune with my writing was never one of my objectives. Fame and revenge, reasonable goals at twenty-five, had lost their sheen as motivators. Attention and love—I suppose no writer of any age ever stops wanting to extort these with her novels, his stories; a few promenades around Reality Park, though, prove that one's work will never yield enough of either. The sharp, exhilarating hunger for achievement that drove my younger self had mellowed, or dissipated, replaced by a sort of blind and faithful practice. Or was it habit? And if I had lost something, what was its name? Entering my six-week solitude, I wanted desperately to kick butt, and had no idea if I was able.

The snag, after a few days' close examination, revealed itself to be a philosophical knot; in my first ending, I had turned to what I wanted to call magical realism, and should have named pure fantasy, to turn the novel and transform those of the characters susceptible to transformation. On a certain picaresque and zany level, it worked, and might with some time and application have been made to work better, but in the silence my children left behind I was able to hear the admonishings of a certain inner voice. Cheap shot, it said. Cop-out, it said. No intercession by supernatural beings allowed. Temper mockery with moral courage. To finish this book properly, you have to know what you believe, it said.

Yeah, right, I said.

But it *was* right.

As I settled into my summer solitude, I discovered a new delight, or reclaimed an old one—a train of thought, once boarded, could run all night, all through the next day, and into the next night with no stops for dinner or to pick up children. Even if the destination were nowhere, even if the tracks ran out, I could keep on riding until I got to the end of the line. I could travel light or hop a new train any time. If one's processes of thought have become the intellectual equivalent of short commuter runs on local trains, a transcontinental trip seems like a great adventure. For about two weeks, I simply rode my thoughts across the landscape, followed as they branched and sometimes backtracked, spurred and climbed and crossed the mountains. I rode through all weathers and at all hours, past vistas so strange and lovely they sometimes made me cry, not just from sadness but with gratitude as well. At last I arrived at a familiar place so long unvisited it seemed quite new; what I believed was pretty much what I always did, but had forgotten. My beliefs were simple, but they were mine.

It can take a long time for what one wants to say to transmogrify into a story one knows how to tell, but in this case, it didn't. It was as if, while one part of my brain was engaged in conscious thought, another part had been silently, concurrently hard at the very different business of making story. As I began to write my way down from the mountaintop, the trail was there. I could not see it all at once but had to trust; every time I rounded a blind corner, the trail reappeared, clear and passable, to bear me on. I suspect every writer has known some times like these, when it feels as if one is not creating, exactly, but more discovering something that already exists, something that, without knowing, she already knows. For four weeks, more or less, I felt that, as long as I got myself to the keyboard and was attentive, my story, my characters, my world would be there, too. At the conjoining of hard work and extreme ease, discipline becomes irrelevant. This is the drug that addicts us, the euphoria we cannot help but seek again.

In four weeks, I wrote more than two hundred pages of strong, supple prose. I finished my comic novel.

II

Every fairy tale I grew up on, every parable, fable, and myth I know teaches us that if we rise to life's challenges, if we pursue our assigned tasks with honor and tenacity, then we will be rewarded. In the admonition "Follow your bliss" seems implicit the promise that if one does so, the result will be—well, greater bliss. I suspect it is almost impossible for a child of Western culture to embrace a purely spiritual, or mystic, idea of bliss, one wholly divorced from considerations of material and psychological well-being; having issued us his good advice, Joseph Campbell was not exactly explicit about what fruits we might expect to harvest if we took it. Perhaps it is vulgar and shortsighted of me to include in my definition of bliss the ability to pay one's debts, to take pride in work well done, to have a gift one has labored to create be graciously received. Perhaps I have not read deeply enough, not listened closely enough to find the stories that console us when our hard work comes to nothing, when our gift is met with indifference, when the bliss-road, faithfully traveled, does not pass Go but dead-ends in the swamp.

Fact: I finished my comic novel.

Fact: To date, no one has yet expressed a desire to publish it. I do not find these bits of data easy to reconcile.

To an either/or mentality, the choices are clear cut. On the one hand, I can conjûre up that swinish philistine, Corporate Commercial American Publishing, with its passion for filthy lucre and its appetite for swill. Here the argument goes something like, My book's a masterpiece and they're too dumb to know it. Alternatively, I can decide that I'm really not a very good writer and my book's a piece of shit. While I have minutely explored each position in the last few months, truth is, they both seem kind of childish. Either one makes me a sad case. Neither one teaches me how to live.

Fact: I owe my editor a mystery novel by the end of June. As I write this, it is the twenty-first of February.

Panic. Hope. An undulant gray sky.

III

Even to the quietest of places, news finds its way.

Within my circle of acquaintance are tales of many novels wandering homeless on the streets of New York, crisp hopeful manuscripts growing more tattered, more disheveled with each submission, each rejection. Rumor extends the circle. What wonders in those shabby boxes? How many broken dreams?

Ticknor and Fields is closing, Atheneum is no more; the list of lost literary imprints grows long. In and around New York, publishing companies are being bought, sold, reorganized at an alarming rate.

The conversion of the gentlemanly occupation of publishing

to business began in the early 1970s, with the acquisition of publishing companies by major corporations whose primary interest in books was confined to those kept by their accountants. The idealistic young editors of 1974 have, of necessity, become the hard-nosed executives of the 1990s; the question underlying a commitment to publish has slowly been transformed from Is this a worthy book? to Can I hit this out of the park? This home-run mentality has left book publishers grasping after that chimerical thing, the One Big Book That Everybody Buys. How on earth can any human, or any committee comprised thereof, reliably predict the wonderful vagaries of public taste? Raising the stakes so high has paralyzed the editorial imagination and staled the appetite for risk.

Editors, my own included, are quitting or losing jobs and scrambling to find new ones. And who can blame the agents who close their doors? The books that do sell, sell for less. Agents' livelihoods are no more certain than their authors' anymore.

Crisis is opportunity, of course. Throughout Western history, the breakdown of cultural institutions tends to stimulate innovation and renewal within the culture itself. The self-destruction of New York as the capital of American literary culture doesn't mean the culture will die, only that it will migrate, diffuse, and reinvent.

Change comes slow, comes hard and hopeful. Change takes its hostages. American letters will survive the transition, I have no doubt.

The question that haunts me is this: How many writers will not?

IV

Berg is a detective. His mother named him Soren, after Kierkegaard, but he rarely uses his given name. Berg is Norwegian. He offices in Ballard. At fifty, divorced, he rides a Harley-

Davidson, needs reading glasses but doesn't like to wear them. He's a gifted athlete, highly competitive, and has a problem with alcohol he's trying to treat by force of will. His daughter Danielle plays varsity high school soccer and, wanting to be a good father, he goes to all her games. On Thursday afternoons, he meets his old friend and football rival Eddie, now a professor at the UW, at the Blue Moon on 45th to drink beer and play a few high-stakes games of darts. Perhaps what interests me most about Berg is that while he feels things deeply, he doesn't think about them. He refuses to live an examined life.

When I sat down last fall to start writing the mystery novel due in June, there was Berg, striding into the Blue Moon almost as if he'd been waiting for me to show up. Third person? It was okay with Berg; he didn't need to hog the limelight, seemed to understand that a mystery flows more easily from multiple points of view. Of course, I recognized odd bits of me and a few of my friends in him, but all in all, Berg seemed to be his own man. He exhibited a wondering willingness to *behave*, a trait which unfailingly endears a character to his author. Berg was new territory, and I liked writing him. Pretty soon, I had a serviceable first chapter and a working title, *Ballard Bitter*, after the local designer beer. My editor, of the middle-aged male persuasion himself, liked both.

Less because the Seattle music scene is "hot" than because I wanted an excuse to check it out for myself, I chose it for the principal venue of my mystery. Across the cut, I planned to write a woman—the mother of the bass guitar player who gets in trouble, a sparring partner and potential love interest for Berg. Damned if she would come. Rather, she was old business, entirely too much like the women who'd figured in my last two novels. Moira—it took three drafts even to find her a name— kept sounding and thinking and acting like Freddy, of *Bones*, or like Judith, who tells all of *Paradise Illustrated* in her own voice. Anyone who's written a few novels recognizes the problem of persisting voices, the need to purge them. Once I saw the problem, I figured I could solve it. I had before.

Moira refused to be solved, just sat there like a huge boulder blocking the entrance to the cave while I beat my head against her. Weeks went by, then months; the drafts piled up and still I didn't have a working chapter two. I continued to do my research, visiting clubs, talking with musicians and other assorted scenemakers; my understanding of the ambience deepened and distant bits of plot flashed into view, but I couldn't make it across that cut until the morning it occurred to me that perhaps the problem wasn't really Moira at all.

I did then what any sensible self-made schizophrenic would— I sat down and had a conversation with my muse. The technique is simple enough; you'll find it or variants in any of the process-oriented how-to manuals. Sit down at the keyboard and assign names to whatever parts of yourself you perceive to be in conflict, tagging each "voice" as if it were a character in a play. Urge them to be candid and forthcoming with one another, then open the dialogue. Stay in character as you write each speaker; don't try to mediate. Most often this exercise is recommended when the editor and writer selves are at odds, interfering with one another's performance. I named my speakers Me and Muse. It was a long time since I'd had any contact, real or imagined, with my muse, a long time since I'd acknowledged the part of me that makes my stories. You might say I'd been neglecting her. That's what she said.

At least that morning, my muse was she, and she was very young, perhaps seven, and very angry. Me didn't have to say much to coax the story out; she was angry because I expected her to work all the time, but never praised her or rewarded her work. She was tired of being asked to support a family and envious of my children, of the attention I give them, the love and care. You have to nag them to take out the garbage, she pointed out. I write two and a half novels, and you don't even say thank you. I come through for you, time and again, and you never even say, Good job. And now you're asking me to do it again.

At this point I was moved, lamely, to defend myself. Hey, it hasn't been exactly easy for me, either.

I work my butt off for you, and at the end, you're all bummed out.

There are reasons—

I don't care if nobody's bought your book, she said. That doesn't matter. Did I do a good job or didn't I?

Yes, honey. You did a good job.

Are you proud of me?

I am.

And do you love me?

Yes. I do.

She was very like my children are sometimes, when they accuse me of expecting too much, or taking them for granted. Perhaps because of them, I could see her little tear-stained face and upraised chin, how tightly she hugged herself to keep from flying apart entirely, could feel how much she hurt and how long this had been coming.

I'm sorry, I said, and then, because I could think of nothing else, I asked her timidly, Would you like me to buy you a present?

She nodded through her tears.

V

At the toy store, we made straight for the stuffed animals. There were four big bins of them, all species, all sizes and colors of plush. The price limit I set, generous but not extravagant, eliminated the larger creatures. She did not want a rabbit or wolf or a kitten. We set to examining the bears, studying their expressions, holding each one and testing the softness of its fur. We were so long at this task the saleslady appeared at my elbow.

Essay: *A Woman, Three Novels, a Muse, and a Bear*

"Perhaps if I knew who you were shopping for, I could help you," she said.

I smiled. "I'm looking for a present for a very special child. I'm sure I'll know it when I see it."

The bear my muse chose, finally, is all white, perhaps eighteen inches from upraised nose to tail, a seated bear with short arms open, small shining gray eyes, just a hint of worry on its white brow, a perpetually good-natured smile. It is soft to stroke and soft to squeeze, just the right size to sit on my lap when I'm writing or reading or watching TV. We have named our bear Calliope, my muse and I. My children think it is peculiar, to see a grown-up carrying a stuffed animal, although they do concede it is a lovely bear.

VI

What happens across the cut is Mitch. He's twenty years old and plays the bass guitar. It's a windy October day in Chapter Two as he strides through Belltown on his way to audition for an unexpected opening in Umbrella, what everybody expects to be Seattle's next big band. He's nervous and excited and full of himself. The audition goes well. The plot is set in motion. When Moira comes in, in Chapter Three, she's tractable and suitably mysterious, doesn't try to take over the novel or tell her secrets all at once. Other characters take shape around these two. The next cut, I think, is back to Berg.

Calliope sits beside me as I write. The clouds have flattened and lifted a little, taken on the slightest tinge of blue. Outside my window, it has begun to rain again.

Elizabeth Logan Harris

*My mother and me (age six months). I have always wanted
to know what was on the other side.*

A native of Lynchburg, Virginia, Elizabeth Logan Harris was educated before,
during, and after time spent earning degrees from Brown University and the
University of Virginia. Her short fiction has appeared in *Mid-American Review,
New England Review,* and *Columbia.*

Harris lives and writes in Cincinnati.

Elizabeth Logan Harris

ELIZABETH LOGAN HARRIS
Golden Feet

Late Friday night when Simon had finished the
Empire sofa for Charlotte Glen's client, he swept the last scraps
off the floor of his shed and carried a box of trash out to the
garbage can on the curb. As he came across his front yard in the
moonlight, Simon appeared much older than his fifty-seven
years. His thin hair, which had lost its original auburn tint and
gone completely white, was combed straight back from his
deeply grooved forehead. He leaned forward as he walked. It
was not, however, the weight of the carton that stooped Simon's
shoulders; his body curved of its own accord. His neck jutted out
and his head tilted downward, a stance which usually sent
Simon's gaze somewhere in the vicinity of his navel, as if the
truth he was destined to ponder were an inward one.

He emptied the contents of the box and returned to his shed,
where he stood admiring his work. Only three weeks before, he
had torn away the crimson remains of the old upholstery and
studied the bare sofa's arched back and sloping lines, with the
same amount of interest that most men reserve for a woman's
backside. The sofa arms curled and rolled under themselves,
reminding Simon of the scrolls he'd seen in Bible illustrations,
decrees of heavenly wisdom tucked for posterity under the
prophet's arm. The fabric, a brilliant royal blue, he had fitted and

tucked with care into the delicately carved frame. The bent and missing upholstery tacks, whose rusty rims had punctured the old fabric, had been replaced with new brass ones; Simon had doggedly spaced out the tacks every three-eighths of an inch along the entire edge of the fabric.

And the wood. Never before had he worked with a fine mahogany, pure heartwood, straight, uniform grain.

Before he began the upholstery, Simon had spent long days in the shed, its thin walls barely keeping back the cold February wind. The space heater glowed a mean orange while he rubbed along the curls and grooves, restoring oils to the old wood, polishing the work of a long-dead craftsman, a picture of whom Simon drew in his mind from time to time. Based on one trip to Colonial Williamsburg and a vague image of Miles Standish, Simon dressed his furniture maker in a Jeffersonian waistcoat and square-buckled shoes. The more intricate the costume he imagined for the craftsman, the more his appreciation grew; the sofa seemed like an even greater achievement when he considered its maker had crouched over a workbench wearing a wig.

When Simon picked up the antique at Fearon's Moving and Shipping, Charlotte Glen (Simon always called her by both names, thinking Charlotte too familiar and Mrs. Glen too formal for someone closer to his daughter Braid's age than his own) met him there and showed him a tattered piece of cobalt-blue cloth that she explained came from the rats' nest. They were still standing in the back lot when she lifted the fabric out of a narrow plastic sleeve. Her voice squeaky and excited, she carefully held the scrap of material—not enough to patch a tear in the seat of his granddaughter's pants—between her forefinger and the tip of her thumb. Charlotte Glen stepped out of the shadow of the building and into the light. "Would you just look at that blue!" she exclaimed in short, quick breaths as though she had managed to cut away a piece of the sky.

At first, Simon was under the impression that "The Rats'

Nest" was the name of a store. You saw names like that nowadays, names that bore no relation—at least none that he could tell—to the things they sold in the store. But she went on to explain that the little bit of frayed blue fabric had been found in a real rats' nest in the wall of the Stewarts' house.

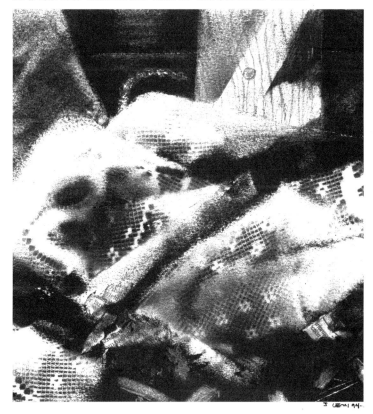

"You know it's original to the house," she said, turning her frosted blonde head from side to side to keep the sun out of her eyes. "They lived at the Stewarts' for over five generations, those rats. And their nest was quite elaborate. Separate compartments for sleeping and eating. Absolutely amazing—they have managed to preserve history better than we! Can you imagine all those years spent just the other side of the dining room wall?"

Simon said he couldn't really.

Charlotte soon returned the blue morsel to its sleeve and began talking about the hand-stitching that would be necessary. Then she produced another envelope which contained a photograph of a sofa similar to the one Simon was hired to cover. "This one is in a museum in Richmond," she said, "English, 1825. Very close to the Stewarts'." Did he see the placement of the tacks? He did. But his mind was hung up on the rats and the material. Surely she didn't mean for him to reconstruct the fabric? His wife Millie couldn't have, she wouldn't have said he was a weaver, too? Would she? As it was, he was thinking that maybe Millie had gotten them in too deep. They could always use the business, but from how Charlotte Glen was talking Millie had promised more than she should have. He had heard her bragging to customers: Simon this, Simon that. "Simon'll have it done faster than you can say Jack Robinson." He hoped Millie hadn't flat-out lied.

"It's just a small area that requires hand-stitching. Try to get as close as you can to this picture," Charlotte said, adding that she would stop by the workshop next week and go over everything again.

Simon cringed when she mentioned coming by the "workshop." That meant the shed. (From a very young age, Simon had knocked sawdust out of his shoes. His mother came from a family of carpenters and coffin makers on the Tennessee-Virginia line. And, apart from his year at the Chilhowie brickworks when he faced the red, hot kiln and flirted with a career in masonry, Simon had, for the better part of his life, preferred wood to people.) Looking down, then at Charlotte Glen's red patent-leathers, he tried not to picture them on the floor of his shed. He just couldn't get used to people in the shed. They left a smell in the place. Smells tended to linger over his workbench, confusing his senses, blocking out the cleaner scents of wood, varnish, and furniture wax; most smells in the workshop were so clearly linked to their origins that he could almost point to a strand of scent that sailed straight through the air to his nose. A rick of pine, an open jar of polish, linseed oil, these put forth distinct smells; never once did they mingle into confusion. But people were spongy; they picked up the odor of where they had been and who they'd been with. Women were the worst. Even Millie's familiar scent, talc mixed with the faint odor of whatever she had last cooked, was always laced with something else, nettling though indistinct. He remembered his mother leaning in the doorway of her father's workshop, her body a clean curve against the violet evening light beyond the door, and how quickly the disconcerting smell of her—rose water, sweat, wild spring onions—penetrated the close, dusty air around him.

What traces of the world would Charlotte Glen leave in his shed? Hair spray, perfume, dry-cleaning fluid? Simon turned back to her. She was putting the photograph back into its envelope. Was he expected to have committed the piece to memory?

He was about to tell Charlotte Glen that she ought to find an upholsterer with more experience, when she said next week she would drop off the bolt of new blue fabric, copied from the rats' swatch (which laid to rest his worries about weaving), and pressed the photograph into his hands. "This is for you to keep," she explained. "A model to go by. The arms are different, but it's the overall shape that I wanted you to see. Those famous tacks, the slope, the lines. That's what we want to achieve: details." Simon clutched the photograph, glad to have something to go by. But it wasn't until some days later when he was in his shed with the sofa and the photograph and a stack of library books on restoration that he felt as though he really understood the task ahead.

In spite of the initial confusion, Simon had done a good job. He still failed to see exactly how the rats entered into it, but considering the success of the finished product—the rich blue against the dark, polished wood—Simon had to allow that if this was what came of rummaging through rats' nests, maybe there *was* something to it. He imagined that you had to be a professional to understand which rats and which nests were (and more important, which weren't) worth unraveling, but he supposed they taught you that in decorator school.

In the cold midnight silence, Simon's pride in his work unfolded. Who would have thought a boy from a house with no more than a stick or two of furniture, and none of that worth a nickel, would have a knack for antiques? He thought proudly of all the reconstruction that was possible in the seclusion of his shed. Charlotte Glen inside the shed had been troubling enough (fingernail polish remover, if he wasn't mistaken), and this whole restoration business seemed over his head, what with its exacting measurements and historical accuracy and finicky society women with shiny red shoes and photographs from museums and some of the damn finest, most silky materials he had ever had the pleasure of touching; but he was dying to do more.

Until recently, his repair and upholstery work had been limited to broken chair legs and threadbare La-Z-Boys. He loved working on these older, finer pieces like the walnut dining table and the wing chair Charlotte Glen had brought to him after Christmas. Being near these beautiful things opened him up somehow, tempted him to look outside himself. Down deep, he couldn't wait to know if his work was good enough. For once, he *cared* to know what people thought about his work, to know how it compared. And this worried Simon. Maybe these odd, new feelings about himself were just another way of trying to measure up. Was he out to prove something, after all? Proving yourself, measuring up—was that all you were left with once you really started to give a damn? Or could it be more than that, deeper still—a dilation of himself and his close world, his very insides seeping out into the light?

Simon tasted blood. He stood up. Leaning against the workbench, lost in thought, he had bitten the dry skin away from his
bottom lip until it bled. As though awakened suddenly, his
movements were abrupt; he cleared off the workbench, hung up
his tools. "The sofa will mean more business," he said aloud.
"That's what matters." That was the side of it he discussed with
Millie. The other was just a foolish notion he mulled over after
too many hours in his shed.

Millie was right when she said where this decorator business
comes from, there's plenty more. "If she likes this one, ask her
if there aren't some more you can do." Why be ashamed of
asking? Millie said getting business was part of business.

Business, yes, business is what I ought to be considering, Simon
thought as he shut off the light and locked the shed. Even though
it was none of Millie's fault, sales in their "Antiques and
Collectibles" store had been slow over the last few years. Millie
always made a few crucial sales at Christmastime, but Simon's
repair work now accounted for more than half of their income.
Folks just didn't seem to be buying like they used to. It crossed
Simon's mind that the decline had, more than anything, to do
with the neighborhood, which, like everything else, had some
age to it now. Most folks on Winter Road had bought about all
the furniture and knickknacks that their houses could hold.
They were starting to give them away to their children and
grandchildren. When he and Millie moved to Perkinsville,
Winter Road was full of families like themselves, a few small
children and the men just getting settled in a line of work. Their
next-door neighbor, Ferris, was starting up his electrician's shop
and Ted Wiley's dress store had only been open a couple of years.
Seemed like everybody needed something in the way of furnishings; there for a while, he and Millie had done well with used
cribs and wicker bassinets along with rockers and dinette sets. As
the families grew older, Simon scoured the tag sales and estate

auctions for desks and junior beds and, before he knew it, the craze was vanity sets for the daughters.

He could recall spending what seemed then like a lifetime pleating material into skirts and attaching them to kidney-shaped vanities. Millie had every teenage girl in the neighborhood wanting a fancy makeup table and Simon thought he would never see the end of those itty-bitty pleats. Millie offered specials on the tables, fifty-five with the fabric, forty without, which meant most people sprang for the skirt. Simon could still remember proud Jackson Powell—tighter than a tick—who bought his girl, Debbie, a vanity but insisted his wife do the covering. Less than a week later, Lila Powell confided to Millie that she would happily pay thirty dollars not to look at a pleat again. And a year or so later, when Millie sent Braid to return the Powells' Rototiller, she came back having seen poor Debbie's vanity shoved against the garage wall. The skirt was only half-finished and what was left of it long since mildewed. Dirty footprints soiled the top. Braid said it looked like somebody had used the vanity as a stepladder.

Walking past the stalky remains of his garden and toward the house, Simon realized Millie wouldn't have a chance to see the sofa in the daylight. She hadn't been down to the shed since the blue material was stretched across the frame; he was sorry to miss hearing her surprise. *Mercy, Simon, that's beautiful!* he imagined her saying. *I didn't know you had it in you! Maybe she'll give you a bonus.* But Millie was leaving before sunrise with Braid and Braid's daughter, Arta. They were going to Pulaski for Millie's sister's birthday.

Simon didn't like women on the road by themselves. "Go on and stay over in Pulaski," Simon had tried to tell them. "I hope you're not going to drive back—"

But Braid broke in, insisting that she had been planning (all along) on carrying Millie over there and back in the same day. "With that cat hair all over everything at Peewee's, Mama won't get a wink of sleep," Braid argued.

Millie had curled her lip and nodded, but Simon figured Braid was probably hurrying back just to spite him; or maybe she had one of her "dates" that would keep her out till all hours. Braid already had one child out of wedlock and Simon figured she'd end up with another before she was through. He had finally conceded: "As long as you are back by dark."

On his way into the house, he noticed the clouds; the white ring of light that shone around the moon could only mean snow. If the snow started falling before they left, he wouldn't let them go. He could refuse to let them go, couldn't he? He made up his mind to speak to them again in the morning. They definitely weren't gallivanting across the state in the middle of a snowstorm. He wouldn't have it.

He crawled in bed beside Millie. She jumped when his feet, cold and stiff from standing in the shed all evening, brushed against her bare calf. "Lord, Simon! Get you some socks on those feet 'fore you catch your death."

Like an animal resigned to a space much too small for itself,

ELIZABETH LOGAN HARRIS

Simon rolled over to his side of the bed, drew himself into a ball, and dozed off.

The morning forecast said winter storms were possible later in the day. Talking to Braid, Simon stressed "possible" as if it meant "likely." Braid said they were wrong half the time anyway and started loading the car. Before she left, Millie said, "Be sure and wrap that sofa up good and tight in the plastic. Shame it can't wait till Monday for delivery. I wanted to get a good look at it. Ask her about doing some more, ya hear?"

"I don't like you out there in the snow," he said one last time, but Millie put her breakfast dishes in the sink and Braid went out to the car. Not even his granddaughter turned around. She went right on eating cereal and staring out the window at the dark.

"Just because it's March, don't think it won't snow," Simon said, standing by the car as Millie put a bag of snacks in the back seat beside Arta. "Y'all be on the lookout. Stay at Peewee's if it starts up. Don't do anything foolish, hear? If you run into it on the way, pull over—"

Millie nodded and waved her hand in dismissal. Braid leaned across her mother's lap and yelled to Simon that she was a grown woman. As if once you turned a certain age, the weather didn't bother with you anymore.

"Got enough for a motel?" Simon called into the crisp dawn air, but the car doors had already been slammed shut.

Later, heading for the shed with big plastic sheets from the basement, Simon thought of Charlotte Glen and her reaction to the sofa. She had complimented him on the armchair upholstery, had been pleased with the walnut table, but if he wasn't mistaken, there were some critical undertones in her praise. She said things like "not bad at all" and "really quite acceptable work," as if she had been expecting something less than acceptable. And when she called to offer him the sofa job, she

128 *Glimmer Train Stories*

said: "I suppose you can handle an Empire piece? I'm in a bind. Polly Stewart has to have the sofa by Sunday, March fourth— for her open house. I'll go over everything with you." There again, Simon detected some doubt bordering on condescension.

When he mentioned the conversation and his feeling about it to Millie, she said: "Nonsense, all of them up on the Avenue talk that way. She's giving us the business, isn't she?" and went right on paging through her great big antique encyclopedia until she got to *Empire*.

Simon didn't think he could stand hearing any snide remarks or criticisms, subtle or not, about *this* sofa. As he wrapped it in the full light of morning, he was more and more sure of what he had suspected the night before: it was a beautiful thing, his best piece of work. He secured the plastic sheets three-deep with masking tape and twine and got his neighbor, Roy, on the phone. He had promised to help Simon load the piece into the truck. Roy said it was as cold as a witch's tit in a brass brassiere, but he would be over in a few.

The icy rain that began almost as soon as Simon pulled the truck off Winter Road and onto Piedmont Avenue beat across his windshield all the way out to the county road, where the conditions were compounded by a fierce wind. He turned off the main road and kept both hands on the wheel, only letting go to turn the dial. He was listening for the forecast, hoping the storm wasn't headed for the Pulaski area. With the sky so dark it was hard to tell. It seemed to be coming out of the north. At any rate, he thought, Braid and Millie should have reached Peewee's a good hour ago.

He glanced down at the directions in his lap and turned again onto a narrow road with low shoulders that sunk into ditches on either side. Nearly all the county roads were like this one: full of hairpins and, in most places, hardly wide enough for two cars to pass. They reminded him of the ones he had run along barefoot as a boy back in Tennessee.

He kept the speed low and honked when he went around the blindest turns. The wind whipped and swirled down from all directions, building up such a force sometimes that the body of the truck jiggled on its wheels. He drove on. No one was on the road; sleet blew against the windshield in curtains of shiny gray.

Just as he came out of a tight curve, a tree on the high bank above the road appeared to be coming straight for him.

Simon thought he must be dizzy. A cedar, thick-trunked and full-branched, was dropping away from the hillside, plowing up the sky.

Stunned, he watched the world tilt toward him; the truck seemed to glide forward as if it were part of a well-timed duet, the tree performing its part in a slow, graceful swoon.

Seconds before the crescendo, he winced. Head down. Hit the brakes. The truck's back end shot out from under him and flung sideways across the road.

The tree was taller—longer—and reached farther than he expected; it was still falling, grasping for the truck and its driver like a sleek, black arm. Just as the tree was about to pierce his windshield, Simon saw a band of, of—small gold creatures— angels. *Angels!*

Their faces glowering under the strain, the angels were lined up along the heaviest bough; they held the tree above his windshield while the truck slid forward, out from under the tree. The cedar landed with an enormous crash behind him, in the truck bed, smack on top of the antique sofa. And the angels were gone.

They hadn't been carrying harps—much too busy to be encumbered with such tall instruments, not to mention all those strings. But angels were what Simon had seen. Behind the wheel, dazed and trembling, he had no doubt about it.

He shook. His hands still gripped the wheel, his eyes blinked back the pattern of light and dark that skittered across his field of vision.

The truck straddled the road. Somehow he had stopped it in midslide. The barbed-wire fence still ran along one side of the road, the underbrush tossed in the wind, the dead leaves that had wrapped themselves around his antenna flapped limply, like battle-worn standards. Nature seemed to have no trouble reordering herself. But all of Simon's senses went on and on and on humming one single note: *You might be dead, Joseph Simon Quincey.* That was the one thing that stood out. *You might be dead.* It flew around in his head, crashed up against the more delicate thoughts, ran harum-scarum through layers of meaningless subtleties; death mowed down all but the simplest notions of time and place.

Out of nowhere! Like miniature weight lifters, arms pressed taut, they had appeared. Saved him.

Simon slumped over the steering wheel and prayed. Long, deep, inarticulate prayers about saviors, redeemers, forces of nature, issued from him in gasps. This was not his usual supplication to the One and Only. Everything in his prayer, howsoever vague and mingling, was plural. Was he wrong to try to speak to the creatures he had seen flying before his windshield, rescuing him? Were they distinct from or part of the Holy Spirit? Were they perhaps bad? Angels of death? Would a price be exacted in return for his life? Such thoughts of fairy-tale destiny paraded through Simon's head; as soon as he caught the tail of one, another knocked him spinning again, no scheme of logic attached.

His grip on the wheel had been so tight that his fingers ached with stiffness. Clusters of small limbs, long strips of bark, twigs still a few weeks away from budding lay up and down the road, snapped off by the same whirling gust that had felled the heavy cedar. Wood shavings were plastered against the windshield now that the wipers were still. He got out and surveyed the devastation in the bed of the truck. Wind cut through his jacket before he could zip it up all the way. At first he thought he could move the limb off the truck himself, but after half a dozen futile heaves and shoves, he saw that it would be impossible to lift. Could he pry it off? There was nothing around to wedge underneath and, besides, he was far too cold and weak for such an effort.

He bent down to get a good look at the sofa. Tangles of branches and their web of fine green needles hid the sofa from view, but he knew it was destroyed. Smashed to bits. Probably more like kindling now than furniture. He had known the sofa's fate even before he had gotten out of the truck. Beneath and among the loud shattering and confusion of the wind and the storm and the frightening collapse of the sky, his ears had somehow been tuned to the smaller sounds. Instead of a single loud boom, he heard only the sleet pelting above him and the gritty sliding of his tires on the pavement and the crinkles of splintering wood.

He decided to let the truck pull itself out. The gusts now were every bit as bad as the blast that had toppled the tree. *I might not be so lucky next time*, Simon thought, getting quickly back into the truck and punching the accelerator. After three or four jerks forward and backward, he managed to rock the truck out from under the weight of the tree. He got out again, daring to look at the damage. The sides of his bed were badly dented. Tears in the plastic covering exposed a sofa beyond repair; the tree had dragged bits of crushed wood and cotton batting off the truck with it.

Millie would want to know about the bill, would they still get paid? He *had* done the work, after all. Was there insurance for things like storms and big heavy trees flying into cars? Or would they classify this an act of God? Simon knew he would have a hard time arguing against that classification.

In the midst of his despair, Simon had a comforting thought: at least now no one can say just how good (or bad) my work on the sofa was. Not my wife, not Charlotte Glen, not even the

Stewarts' party guests. As Simon collected scraps of the sofa from the wet asphalt, a calm smile spread over his face.

Out from under the tree, the truck bounced forward. He looked for a place to turn around. He would go home now. The sofa was of no use to anyone. *Back home*, he thought, *I'll know what to do next.* And then he remembered the feet. They had golden feet. Were there gowns? He hadn't noticed gowns, only the tight, determined faces and small buttery feet. Their arms had stretched out and caught the tree, held it there just long enough. Millie would claim he was having a low-sugar fit, that he had eaten too little breakfast, or too much. But he knew Arta would believe him if he told her about the angels. With all that they were finding out now—men in outer space, waves and tubes and lights all sending signals, everything plastic—it seemed to Simon just a matter of years before they came up with an explanation for everything, before they understood angels or science was able to reason them away. He would go home now. He would hold his granddaughter and tell her how there really was such a thing.

Simon looked down the road and then through the mirror behind him. Still nothing coming in either direction. His eyes followed a fence that started around the last bend and led up to the top of a small knoll a half mile or so down the road. He could see the front gate of the place where the fence arched up and receded down the other side of the slope. The fence was well tended; not a stretch of it that he could see needed paint. He turned into the gate and backed around in the other direction. A well-kept fence meant a big, freshly dusted home somewhere there in the middle, hemmed in by the fence, cushioned by all that land. His eyes followed the fence until it trailed out of sight over the next hill and appeared again at the crest of a far knoll.

As a boy, Simon had known a place with a fence like that. The

Swanson place, a big farm not far from where he grew up. His
mother was a friend of the tenant family and he was allowed to
fish in the farm pond. His father, who had walked out when
Simon was barely eight, had first talked to him about fishing.
"Have to have patience, son. Fish don't come if you don't wait
for them." And though Simon never caught much—a snapping
turtle, a perch or two—he liked to wait. Liked to sit afternoons
on the rickety dock where he could see the sandy bottoms of his
dangling feet reflected in the water. Only once had he gotten a
big fish out of the Swansons' pond. He was almost twelve. His
mother said she was spending the afternoon at the Swansons'
place and he could take his pole along.

"You fish here a while. I'm going up to see Wanda at the
tenant house. Catch me something big. Don't go wandering off
or coming up to bother me and Wanda. Behave now, and we'll
see about buying you that reel and all. I'll holler for you when
I'm ready to leave." Simon wondered where she would find
money for a new rod and reel. He watched her climb the hill;
she had on pink lipstick and a flower-print dress that he had
never seen before.

Simon worked the slippery worm over the hook and wet his
line. It was a windy April day and his second cast landed on the
bank; he spent a good half hour trying to free the hook from the
tangles of a wild blackberry thicket. Then, settling back down
on the dock, wetting his line again, a big one took hold. Simon
pulled it in. A largemouth bass, fat and pretty, brown speckles on
its sides, silvery underneath. Excited, he dashed up the hill
toward the barn and the tenant house in search of his mother.
The bass flapped fiercely on the end of the pole, its tense, white
jaw open wide as it gasped for water. The front door of the
tenant house was locked and the barn was empty. Simon shoved
open the heavy door to the stable beside the barn. There on a
bench to one side of the door, he saw his mother's bare legs
spread around the shape of what had to be Mr. Swanson. A short,

ugly troll of a man with a gruff, powerful voice—he had hollered at Simon once about leaving trash on the dock.

Simon recognized the scar on his mother's knee, a mark in the shape of a U that she had once told him came from being toppled in a wheelbarrow, but had said more recently that it was caused by a razor blade. He hadn't pointed out the contradiction in her stories; he was still deciding which one to believe.

Before the couple could untangle themselves, Simon ran. Still gripping his fish in one hand and his pole in the other, he headed for the woods. At the edge of a clearing, he collapsed against a tree and lay there looking high up into the branches of a slender beech. Way up there, flapping in the wind, Simon saw something white. It was caught on a bough. He kept his eyes on it, whirling in the air, wild and confused, trying to pull loose one minute and then falling back against the tree, covering the branch like a silky cloak. Was it a flag or a kite? It looked most like a sheet off somebody's line. As Simon watched the white fluttery thing, grief unfurled slowly from the bottom of his throat in tight, angry sobs. "Mama," he said aloud, a name he hadn't used since he was very small. Instead, he called her Ma, which seemed now like a little grunt of a name for someone who mattered so much. A long, sad "Maaa—ma" came out, then another. "Mama," he cried, mad and hurt. "Mama." The dead fish, a slick green crescent, fell from his hand into the blades of new grass at his side. Its gills were flared wide, exposing fans of delicate red netting beneath the flaps.

Simon lay beneath the tree a long, long time and watched the lovely white dancer above him. Obeying only the wind, the sheet rippled up and out, up and away. He let the fish and the pond and the brutish figure of Swanson float up in the tree, let them fly away on the sheet and the air. For years, Simon guarded the image of that tree and its billowing veil; he kept it close and recalled it often until it became more vivid, more beautiful and necessary than the scar on his mother's knee.

Simon called Charlotte Glen as soon as he got home.

"Beyond repair?" She was disbelieving. "Are you sure? Do you realize what a piece of furniture like that is worth?"

Simon said he knew very well, had seen the price on the auction invoice. "I was lucky, very lucky I wasn't killed."

"Oh my, yes! I'm so glad nothing happened to you. It must have been terrifying. That you aren't harmed, that is the main thing. What will Polly say? Devastated. I'm sure she'll be completely devastated. Could I come over there and have a look? Oh, but we've got a dinner thing tonight—in an hour— how about tomorrow? In the morning, before church. Would that be all right? I think I should look at it so I can explain to Polly. Oh dear, I suppose *I* have to call her now. Oh, all that gorgeous fabric—not a piece left?"

"About a yard or so, but I don't see how—" Simon said.

"All right. How about nine tomorrow morning? I'll be over there then."

Simon ignored the fact that Braid and Millie returned from Peewee's an hour after dark. Once they had unloaded the car, he told them about the accident and brought everyone outside to see. Huddled around the back of the truck in the cold, they looked on as he pointed out the soggy ruins. Millie gasped and looked away from the truck, shaking her head. "You might have been hurt something serious, Simon," she said. "Lord have mercy, I'm glad you are in one piece, Honey." He was about to tell her how it really had been close, how, if not for the angels, their strength, when she went on, "It's not like you didn't do the work. She'll have to take that into account. What a shame. Can't be helped, I suppose. No, not in a million years—hmm, hmm. No siree, all the king's horses, all the king's men, not in a million. When you talk to Mrs. Glen tomorrow, see if you can't be paid for it anyway. Some of it, at least. Come on in the house and let's get you some dinner."

After dinner, Simon decided to tell them exactly how it

happened; matter-of-fact, nothing theatrical, no mystery, just come right out with it, that was the best way. "There were some awful high winds and freezing rain, and the tree came falling right for me. But, thing was, you see, there were angels. All these little angels lined up along the tree and kept it in the air. Nothing happened to me because they were holding up the tree. The cab moved forward, see, under the tree. Then they disappeared and the tree fell right on the sofa. They had these tight little faces, and golden feet—"

"Arta, you run along, Honey. Get in your pajamas. We've had a long day," Millie said, shooing her granddaughter out of the kitchen. "Hush that foolishness before Arta hears you," she said, turning back to Simon.

That Millie and Braid might try to explain it away—weather, lack of sugar, the light, the sky, overworked—these things had occurred to Simon. But that they would think he wasn't telling the truth, would accuse him of lying to his own family, say he made the angels up, that he should be careful talking such foolishness around his granddaughter, that didn't cross his mind until he saw the little hunk of skin dangling from the back of Braid's throat, her mouth stretched wide with laughter.

Simon sat up late that night. There was no use going into it any further with Millie or Braid. He saw that. He would keep the angels to himself, away from the careless eyes and ears of other people. Maybe one day when Arta was older he would explain to her just what he had seen.

Simon would see the angels again. They would come to him, as splendid and untiring as they had first appeared against the sliver of stormy sky: when Braid walked back in the house after three months of marriage, her nose broken and bloody, Arta behind her in tears; when a teenage Arta was driven home in a police car after she had been caught naked in the middle of the night on the floor of a vacant house in the arms of a young man;

when, after Millie's stroke and her stay in the hospital, Simon wheeled her to the front window and, in the unbearable stillness, lifted the first spoonfuls to her mouth; when, at the age of seventy-four, on a cold November morning, Simon felt a squeeze of pain in his chest and had a second to marvel at the coincidence before he slumped over a bolt of material, as brilliant blue a fabric as he had seen since the Empire sofa.

But that night in his dark house, Simon had no inkling of these events to come. He grew sleepy and went to bed. Millie was hunched down, well under the warm sheets. She complained of his chilly feet as she had the night before. Instead of drawing them back, though, Simon edged his toes under Millie's nightgown and up between her soft, full thighs, pressed together as she slept on her side. She mumbled another groggy protest, but let them stay. He made one more tentative foray—higher and deeper between her legs—until (he was surprised to discover) the tips of his toes grazed the ends of her pubic hair. In the haze of early slumber, Simon's thoughts alternated between wondering when Millie had stopped wearing underpants to bed and imagining that he was suspended over a flying carpet, his feet barely touching the plush, woolen weave as it coursed through the air.

A writer who can do five pages
even on a bad day is a plugger.

Frank Ronan

*I have absolutely no memory of this photograph being
taken, but I suppose it shows one might have been
happy from time to time.*

Frank Ronan, a young Irish writer, has had three novels published: *The Men
Who Loved Evelyn Cotton, A Picnic in Eden,* and *The Better Angel.* The first won
him the *Aer Lingus/Irish Times* Irish Literature Award. In the United States, it
was also published by Pantheon. Ronan's new novel, *Dixie Chicken,* will be
published in 1995 by Hodder in the United Kingdom.

FRANK RONAN
The Rower

You take the road from New Ross toward Kilkenny and cross the Barrow at Mount Garret Bridge, and turn right by the gray house on the corner as if you were going to Graiguenamanagh, and if you are not driving too fast you will find yourself passing through The Rower, where you might notice the scattering of houses along the main road, but you will see no people. You will need to ask directions to find the house of Lily Stevens, so it is best to go into the shop, if it is open, and ask there. They will send you toward her by rough lanes and complicated turnings and, no matter how well you understand the directions, you will be lost once or twice. Be prepared for reversing in narrow dead ends with your back wheels spinning in the heavy mud. There was one memorably wet winter when Lily Stevens's husband had to pull the harvester through the fields with a bulldozer to save the sugar beets.

The house is almost square and covered with a lattice of dormant Virginia creeper. The front door faces a small garden surrounded by a low wall and intersected with neglected bushes of acrid box. In the damp air, it is this smell of box which dominates the garden. The door is painted yellow and has not been opened within the span of my memory. Drive into the yard at the back and let yourself in through the porch door, past the rusting, humming freezer and into the kitchen. You may find someone there to make yourself known to, and you might not.

Glimmer Train Stories, Issue 12, Fall 1994
© 1994 Frank Ronan. All rights reserved.

Lily Stevens's son and his family live in a bungalow they have built on the other side of the haggard.

There is not much time left. It has been known for some weeks now that Mrs. Stevens is near death, and most of the people who would have done so have come to The Rower to take their leave of her. And prepare yourself. She is so far gone now that she may not recognize you, and you may find it disturbing to hear the noise she makes as she tries to breathe, small and lost in the middle of her bed. She doesn't really speak anymore because of the effort it takes to get the words from her brain to her mouth through the fog of painkillers. Her last words have yet to be recorded, but she has had her last conversation.

"Don't just stand there," she said. "Come and sit by me."

There was no chair, so I made a place for myself among the newspapers and dictionaries and old Penguin paperbacks on the end of the bed, and sat on the pattern of small pink flowers that covered her quilt. Under my weight, the bed groaned and the old feathers made a sigh of compaction.

"I didn't think you'd know me," I said.

A flicker of humor passed across her face. She had never been someone who tolerated false modesty and so, between us, a statement such as the one I had just made could only be taken as a joke. All the same, it was three years since I had last been home, since I had last seen her, and then we had only had the briefest of conversations, in the middle of the street in New Ross. She was still sprightly then, young for her eighty years, still driving herself into town once a week to do her shopping. She had made me promise that I would come out to The Rower to see her before I went away again. I had broken my promise, and I still remember the guilt I felt as the plane flew south from Dublin over the deadening cloudscape that passed for a view.

The bed creaked again with some small movement I made.

"You have a good color," she said. "Are you still in the same place?"

"I've just moved to Lisbon. But the climate's the same."

"Lisbon," she said.

She was silent for a few moments, not as though she had nothing to say, but more as though she were taking a little rest before continuing. I read the spines in the bookcases while I waited.

She said, "I have a book of Portuguese poetry somewhere there. I can't remember the man's name, but I suppose you know it anyway. Not good, but very earnest."

She looked over at her bookshelves, somewhat helplessly.

I said, "It tends to be a bit like that. I think the Portuguese have been brutal for so long that, since the revolution, they have found that there is nothing left in them but goodness and earnestness."

"It sounds very dull," she said.

"It would be," I said, "if it were true."

She began to laugh at that, but the pain that was brought upon her at the beginnings of laughter was so great that it defeated her amusement.

After a little while, I read the clues of the *Irish Times* crossword to her and wrote in the answers she gave. The crosswords of the previous few days were on the bed, each one filled in by the hand of a different visitor.

"You haven't married yet?" she said.

"No."

"I never thought you would."

There was no need to give her more information. From the tone of my one word of denial she had divined more than I could divulge.

I was nine years old when I first came into her sphere of influence. She was my schoolteacher for two years. I can't remember any lesson that she taught me, but I can remember having conversations with her in the classroom, talking with her as though the two of us were alone and the thirty other children around me had faded into the gloss-painted walls. I can remember the day I handed her an essay and, after she had read it, she sent one of the children next door to fetch Sister Philomena. Sister Philomena was head of the school at the time, and our days were punctuated by the screaming which came through the glass and wooden folding partition between her classroom and ours. The children under this nun's care had a cowed look about them and scarlet palms where she had beat them with her leather. Because of the noise from next door we were aware, every day, of the good fortune we had to be taught by Mrs. Stevens, whose voice was seldom raised and whose hand never came down on ours in anger.

The messenger returned, followed by Sister Philomena. At the sight of the nun, clutching her leather in the pocket of her apron, my flesh turned to molten tar and my teeth began to chatter with fear. The nun scanned the classroom and rested her eyes on me, knowing by my terror that I was the one for whom she had been called. She drew her leather out as she addressed Mrs. Stevens in harsh Irish.

I tried to review all the words I had put in the essay to know where I had transgressed. I couldn't think what sin I had committed that was so grave it made Mrs. Stevens summon the head, a thing she had never had cause to do before. My eyes were fixed on the leather in the nun's hand. The leather was an instrument known to all schoolchildren of the time, since it was invented and manufactured for their punishment and no other reason. Sister Philomena had refined hers by splitting it down the middle for half its length, doubling the pain it could inflict.

We were standing as the nun entered, out of respect, as we were obliged to do. As Mrs. Stevens handed her my essay she commanded us to sit down. My legs were too weak to sit down in a controlled way, and I hit the seat with a thud. That was when I looked at Mrs. Stevens and saw that she was smiling at me, not just with reassurance, but with pride.

After the reading, Sister Philomena and Mrs. Stevens had a short discussion. Since they were speaking Irish, as all teachers were obliged to do in front of their pupils, I could only understand one word in ten, but I caught enough of it to know that it was complimentary and that it concerned me. Then the nun bid us good morning and we all rose to our feet again, and just before she swept out of the room she gave me a big condescending smile.

Years later I asked Lily Stevens why she had shown the nun that essay. It was after Lily had retired and after I had left school, in the days when I used to cycle out to The Rower to spend the afternoon with her on Sundays, drinking tea and talking about poetry.

Lily said, "I had to show her how intelligent you were. I knew, if I did that, she would never put you in her own class. She didn't like pupils who might be a match for her. I didn't want her to be beating the spirit out of you."

And it was true: before Lily told me that, I had always assumed that in all the class-and-teacher permutations of my time at school it was luck that had kept me away from Sister Philomena and the lick of her leather.

Lily Stevens was the daughter of two schoolteachers, and her mother's parents were both schoolteachers before that. And they had all spent their whole lives teaching in the same school in the same town. So that, for many years, it was said that there was no native of New Ross who had not come under the tutelage of one of that family. Lily had broken with tradition by marrying a farmer, and, since none of her children had shown any interest in becoming a teacher, she was, in some respects, the last of her line.

On her bookshelves, there was a first edition of *Ulysses*, which Joyce had sent to her mother. The parish priest of the time had come to hear of the existence of the book and instructed Lily's mother to burn it. To save a scandal, the book had to be hidden and had to be read in secret. Lily's father was an amateur Greek scholar who had made his own translation of Pindar. This also had to be kept a secret from the town, since it was that part of the *Pythian Odes* which rejected immortality in favor of possibility. They had less clandestine possessions, too: letters to various family members from Yeats and Synge and Mahaffy, letters that were reduced to tattered shreds from being read and reread.

There were times in the life of the town when Lily's family seemed to be the only thread of life running through the town. Times when the state was young and, for want of an identity, it allowed De Valera to impose his ideal of the Irish as an innocent peasantry by repression and censorship; times when the thugs of the old IRA were allowed to swagger unchallenged, before the new IRA made that acronym shameful. There were others, of course, with the courage to think for themselves. But, by and large, they went away, to fight in Spain, to live in Russia, to labor in North London, to teach Portuguese children the English language in my own case. It was Lily's family who stayed behind and kept the thin-spun thread of the intellect running through our town. Perhaps there were others, but that is the family I know of.

"I failed with you," she said. She said this to me as she lay on her deathbed, after she had finished the crossword, after I had said twice that I must be tiring her, that I should be going.

"I failed with you. I wanted you to become a writer, not a teacher."

"That's my own fault. Not yours."

That look she gave me was skeptical. She knew and I knew. It was because of knowing her that I had come to consider teaching to be the higher calling of the two. Perhaps if I had been beaten by Sister Philomena: that might have made a writer of me, a solitary introspective, each thuck of the typewriter keys a blow of the leather returned to the nun.

I tried to justify myself. "There are too many mediocre writers in the world and not enough good teachers. Hardly any good teachers at all."

"Good or bad you might be," she said. "Mediocrity isn't in you."

She said that she wanted her pills, and gave me instructions, and I took a pill from each of five bottles on her bedside table, and held her head, and gave them to her in the right order, one by one, with a sip of water between each. The back of her head was soft and light. I realized that, in all the years I had known her, it was the first time I had touched her. I thought of all the lovers I had touched more intimately who had not known me so well.

After the pills, after I had replaced her head on the pillow as

FRANK RONAN

if it were an unconnected object, she closed her eyes, and I
wondered if she had gone to sleep. I waited some minutes,
standing by her head, thinking I should go and leave her to rest.
I knew that this was our last conversation, and that was why I
hesitated. I moved my feet.

"No," she said. "Don't go. I'm not finished."

I sat again on the tracery of pink flowers on the quilt and the
bed groaned again under my weight. She smiled.

Without opening her eyes, she said, "You're getting to the age
when you should be minding your weight. Wait till you're like
me and you have your work cut out keeping an ounce of flesh
about you."

"Fat chance," I said.

She opened her eyes.

It must have been the drugs. When she opened her eyes there
was an urgency and a vitality in them.

"You're back," I said.

"I'm back," she said.

She said, "Did you notice my agave? On the windowsill."

"Yes?" I said. Although I hadn't noticed the plant before, I had
turned around as she spoke and seen it: it was a spiny star in a pot,
eighteen inches across like any other agave on a windowsill.

She said, "You wouldn't think it was twenty years old. I
brought it back from Portugal when it was a tiny offshoot. If I'd
left it where it was, it would be seven feet wide by now. It might
have flowered and died this summer. I was only in Portugal the
once and the thing I loved most was the sight of flowering
agaves. Monocarpic, is that what you call it? They wait and they
grow and, when they are ready, they throw a flower twenty feet
into the sky. And then, of course, they die. What else could they
do? But this one, this unfortunate on the windowsill: this one can
only get older and older until it dies of oldness. This is the wrong
climate for flowering."

The thing I said next, the answer I gave, was said with a streak of cruelty in it, with a streak of truth in it. I said: "It isn't a question of climate. It is a question of treatment. Physiology is applicable, even in The Rower."

And her answer was: "I knew you wouldn't fail me."

She said, "I am going to die, and I am not going to die without saying this to someone, and it is just as well you are here because, of the people I know who are still living, you are the best person I can tell it to. And don't flatter yourself: it is only because I know that you are someone who will write it down. Things must be written down. If Pindar had never written it down, a thousand people might have thought the same thing since and not known that they had thought it. You might consider yourself Jungian, but only because Jung wrote it down instead of keeping it to himself. There you have the greatest contradiction imaginable. If he had such faith in the collective mind, why did he need to tell anyone what he thought? Never mind. The only thing I have to tell you after eighty-three years, after teaching thousands of children to read and write, after reading Shakespeare and Yeats to rows of children's heads, after teaching my own children to use the lavatory and hold their knives in their right hands and their forks in their left, after loving one man exclusively from his youth to his death, the only thing I have to tell you is something you know already and haven't realized. I'm offering you a shortcut so that you can know this now and not wait, like me, until you are a skeleton on your deathbed. The only thing I have to tell you is that almost everyone you will ever meet on this green earth is someone who has spent their whole life with their head stuffed up their backside."

Having said this, she left a gap for my astonishment and looked at me with drug-wide-opened eyes, challenging me to contradict her. I said nothing.

"Head-in-the-arse is the human condition," she said, as though the vulgarization of her philosophy would penetrate further.

I said nothing.

She closed her eyes for four minutes, and, when she opened them again, she said, "I know what you are thinking. This is an easy thing to say. Anyone could come to the same conclusion after a casual observation of the human race. You can talk to almost anyone and conclude that the only thing you are thinking is that it is the fault of their nurturing; that every human is an extraordinary creation who could be a Mozart or a Sophocles if they hadn't been irreparably damaged by their upbringing. Once upon a time I thought the same thing. I lived by the same creed. I became a teacher, not because my parents were teachers, but because I thought I could draw the Prometheus out of every child, without liver damage. It was when I had my own children that I realized I had been wrong. I loved them and I taught them and they grew up with their heads stuffed up their arses. And then I began to have pupils like you. You weren't the only one. You came to me from stupid parents, but still you had the intelligence to see the world around you. Before I ever met you. Before I had the chance to draw it out of you, you knew it already. I kept you from Sister Philomena so that you could write things down. If the only reason for not writing it down is your fear of mediocrity, then I have failed you. And the thing that damns you to hell is that you have failed yourself."

When she had said all this she closed her eyes again, but this time it was unconsciousness which closed her eyes. I waited, to be sure she had nothing more to say. Dusk fell in the room. Her daughter-in-law came to see to her needs and I left.

There is still time. You can still go to The Rower and take your leave of her, but she has had her last conversation. She has exhausted the realm of the possible. And I have written it down.

The Last Pages

J. LEON 94 —

STEVE ADAMS

*T*his is a picture of Linda's ranch in west Texas. She's a painter and has been abstracting and putting this extraordinary landscape to canvas all of her life. But about ten years ago, the Texas Radioactive Waste Authority chose to put a nuclear waste dump near her family's ranch. She and her sister, Bonnie, a sculptor now working out of New York, did extensive research, pulled in several geologists, and were able to raise enough questions to stop that project. Round 1. Since then, Linda and a literal handful of locals from west Texas, always on the brink of total defeat, have weathered attack after attack for over a decade.

The fight goes on, and I continue to hear the horrifying details of each battle. I can't help but be sorry for how much of Linda's personal and artistic life has been stolen by this war. Truthfully, I'm glad it's not my fight. But it also has taught me how powerful local activists can be. These two women had no training in this area. All they were, and all they consider themselves to be, are visual artists. I wonder, across this country, how many ranchers, shop owners, schoolteachers are engaged in similar fights and are, even if for a short while, winning battles against hugely superior forces.

152   *Glimmer Train Stories*

The function of a writer
is that of a fifth columnist.
The skill is that of infiltrating
the mind of the reader, by
charm; by storytelling: there
to plant an incendiary device.
The explosion may happen
immediately, or there may be
a time-delay. The seeds within
the human brain are
constructed like those in
the Australian bush — they
will only germinate after
fire.

MONICA WOOD

*M*y father, and my mother's parents, were born and raised on Prince Edward Island, Canada, a place of legend and tall tales if ever there was one. I grew up loving ghost stories, and my mother was a bit psychic herself. My father's niece is a professional psychic who investigates houses much the way my character Molly does.

The germ of this story is over ten years old. A friend was taking an adult-ed course at our local university and invited me to visit a class. The instructor was a well-known psychic named Alex Tannous, a magnetic, fascinating man, who, I am sad to say, is no longer with us. (Or is he?) The instant I walked into that class, I knew he was going to call upon me to do something, and my experience was a milder version of what happens to my character Andrew.

Of course, fragments like these do not a story make. This is a story about grief, not ghosts.

One more thing, speaking of psychics—I often wonder if other writers experience what I have come to call *literary prescience*. My fiction is almost never autobiographical, and yet what I write about often ends up happening to me, sometimes months or years after the final draft. It's spooky.

MELANIE BISHOP

*M*y story "Sisterhood" celebrates the relationship I've had with my closest friend, Mary. When she was six and I was seven, her family, full of kids, moved in two doors down from where we lived. There was a girl named Peggy who was seven, like me. One night when I was bored and lonely, my mother suggested I invite Peggy to spend the night. When I called, it turned out that she was already sleeping over at someone else's house. But there were several daughters, and their mother asked my mother if I might like to invite Mary, a year younger, instead. I was open to this substitution, and a few minutes later Mary knocked on the door, holding her pajamas inside a pillowcase. A friendship was born; we have our mothers to thank. Now, thirty years later, with half a country between us, we're still best friends, though we drink coffee more than Icees these days, and neither of us frequents convenience stores any more than the average person. This photo of us was taken last summer after a trip through southern Mexico. Mary's the one looking at the camera.

JIRI KAJANË
KEVIN PHELAN & BILL U'REN

A number of years back, I had the opportunity to travel outside Albania and observe a facility in the Greek town of Thessaloniki. My friends and co-workers were envious of this sudden good luck, and expended a great deal of energy advising me of the many things I should see abroad. Instead, however, I spent all of my free time devising this peculiar tale. Discounting the obstructed view from a taxi window, my entire tour of Greece covered only a few hundred meters.

Upon my return, I did not have the heart to explain how I had foolishly wasted my time. I simply played along with everyone's questions—lying at length about the beautiful Greek city and its many cultural offerings—and, in the process, became the local expert on Greek travel.

As for the story itself, well, I've never known anyone like Leni, although I have always wanted to.

We first met at UCLA under the guidance of Professor Thomas Eekman. At present, we have finished translating one-third of Jiri's collection *Sa Kushtón (What Is the Cost?)*, including "Leni Calls Me for Advice" as well as the stories "Nervous Habits," "This Past Tuesday," and "Wake Up, It's Time to Go to Sleep."

Translators Bill U'Ren and Kevin Phelan

156   *Glimmer Train Stories*

WILLIAM LUVAAS

he only true autobiography is fictitious. Thus, I am at a loss in writing any "truth" about myself. I recall that my mother's hair was brown (or perhaps roan) when I was a boy; my father's face resembled the one I now see before me in the mirror (but beardless). My brother and I were buddies—my sister, too, when we weren't brawling. We loved leaping into icy Oregon lakes and getting out again even better. I was a fan of the University of Oregon's football team—which mostly lost—learning from those huge men who filed somberly past our admiring eyes at game's end as we boys asked for their chin straps, that the Great American Winner's myth is the greatest fiction of all. They lost hopelessly, yet seemed no smaller for it.

It was my wife, Cindy, who emboldened me to write. It seemed to me too audacious a task: to reinvent the truth. But I soon understood there is no choice. Better to invent a good lie than to be invented by it. It is perhaps the creed of fiction to believe that the one will stand in for the other.

ELIZABETH LOGAN HARRIS

I grew up in a family of women. Six generations of us have lived in the same house. And in the South, where there are women there is almost always conversation. Much of what I write about comes from the conversations among women that I have heard or overheard—from my grandmothers, my mother, my sisters, my aunts, my friends, and from the stories of the black women who worked in their houses and cared for me. Whether these stories are literally true doesn't matter; they are the truth I was told.

My father, too, is a great talker, an amateur magician, and an impromptu stand-up comedian. Lately, he has started to draw. The drawing below is one of his. This is his version of women talking. "Golden Feet" is my version of a man who lives in a world of women. Where there are so many women and so much conversation, perhaps angels are necessary.

$\mathcal{P}$AST CONTRIBUTING AUTHORS
Issues 1 through 11 are available for eleven dollars each.

Robert A. Abel • Susan Alenick • A. Manette Ansay •
Margaret Atwood • Kyle Ann Bates • Richard Bausch • Robert
Bausch • Charles Baxter • Ann Beattie • Barbara Bechtold •
Cathie Beck • Corinne Demas Bliss • Valerie Block • Danit
Brown • Gerard Byrne • Jack Cady • Carolyn Chute • Dennis
Clemmens • Tiziana di Marina • Stephen Dixon • Michael
Dorris • Siobhan Dowd • Mary Ellis • James English • Louise
Erdrich • Daniel Gabriel • Louis Gallo • Kent Gardien • Ellen
Gilchrist • Peter Gordon • Marina Harris • David Haynes •
Ursula Hegi • Andee Hochman • Jack Holland • Linda Hornbuckle
• David Huddle • Stewart David Ikeda • Lawson Fusao Inada •
Elizabeth Inness-Brown • Charles Johnson • Wayne Johnson •
Elizabeth Judd • Hester Kaplan • Wayne Karlin • Thomas E.
Kennedy • Lily King • Maina wa Kinyatti • Marilyn Krysl •
Frances Kuffel • Anatoly Kurchatkin • Jon Leon • Doris Lessing
• Christine Liotta • Rosina Lippi-Green • R. Kevin Maler • Lee
Martin • Eileen McGuire • Gregory McNamee • Katherine Min
• Mary McGarry Morris • Abdelrahman Munif • Sigrid Nunez
• Joyce Carol Oates • Vana O'Brien • Mary O'Dell • Peter
Parsons • Jonathan Raban • Anne Rice • Roxana Robinson •
Stan Rogal • Elizabeth Rosen • Janice Rosenberg • Kiran Kaur
Saini • Libby Schmais • Amy Selwyn • Bob Shacochis • Evelyn
Sharenov • Floyd Skloot • Barbara Stevens • William Styron • Liz
Szabla • Abigail Thomas • Randolph Thomas • Joyce Thompson
• Patrick Tierney • Patricia Traxler • Kathleen Tyau • Michael
Upchurch • Daniel Wallace • Ed Weyhing • Lex Williford •
Gary Wilson • Terry Wolverton • Christopher Woods • Celia
Wren

Anxiously awaiting the next issue!

I didn't leave for just that reason. It's only in novels that people do things for one or two reasons. In life we do things for twelve, thirteen, fourteen reasons and the other reasons we've forgotten.

from an interview with Peter Carey by Kevin Bacon and Bill Davis

I cannot decide whether I'm worried about my mother or myself, but I think that there is not much of a difference either way. I go to her and kiss her cheek, and there is the taste of sweat and face cream.

from "A Proper Burial" by Victoria Lancelotta

Artemisa watched her husband pick at the cake, fastidiously separating the layers so that he could scrape away more of the cream filling with the edge of his fork. "But what are you doing, viejo?" she exclaimed. "You think an extra pound or two on that old carcass matters to me? Enjoy yourself, amor. It's our anniversary."

from "The Beautiful Wife" by George Rabasa

I think about that all the time. I'm afraid I'll end up in some flophouse, eating cat food, watching soap operas, nervous to leave my apartment because somebody might take my Social Security check. There are no guarantees. I wish there were guarantees, but there aren't.

from an interview with Christine Turner by Linda Davies